Butch

Also by Kim Antieau

Novels
The Blue Tale
Broken Moon
Church of the Old Mermaids
Coyote Cowgirl
Deathmark
The Desert Siren
The Fish Wife
The Gaia Websters
Her Frozen Wild
Jewelweed Station
The Jigsaw Woman
Mercy, Unbound
Ruby's Imagine
Swans in Winter

Short Story Collections
Trudging to Eden
The First Book of Old Mermaids Tales
Tales Fabulous and Fairy
Entangled Realities (with Mario Milosevic)

Nonfiction
Counting on Wildflowers: An Entanglement
*The Salmon Mysteries: A Guidebook to a
Reimagining of the Eleusinian Mysteries*

Cartoons
Fun With Vic and Jane

Butch

a bent western

Kim Antieau

For Dean &
Kris —
Enjoy!

Much love,

Kim
Antieau 7/10

Ruby Rose's Fairy Tale Emporium • 2012

Butch: A Bent Western
by Kim Antieau

Copyright © 2012 by Kim Antieau

ISBN-13: 978-1468054996
ISBN-10: 1468054996

Cover photos by Kim Antieau.
Book design by Mario Milosevic.

Special thanks to Nancy Milosevic,
Beth Cruz, and Ruth Ford Biersdorf.

Electronic editions of this book are
available at most e-book stores.

A production of
Ruby Rose's Fairy Tale Emporium
Published by Green Snake Publishing
www.greensnakepublishing.com

www.kimantieau.com

To all my kickstarter supporters:
Your affection for Butch inspired me
to keep telling her story.
Thank you!

Joanna Powell Colbert
Beth Cruz
Kristi Tullos
Conni St.Pierre
Jerilee Auclair
Gail Nickel-Kailing
Maggie Lukowski
Jord Creations
Carlee O'Dell
Michael Bourret
Michael Jasper
Cynthia Dominik-Medlin
Patricia Monaghan
Nancy Milosevic
Agica Milosevic
Ruth Ford Biersdorf
Tracie Jones
Jo Ann Albrecht
MaryKate Meyer
Barbara Strasburger
Elaine Massie
Brandi Downs
Nell
Jamie Wede

One

In or around Santa Tierra, New Mexico,
1918 C.E. or thereabouts,
Space and Time being a continuum and all

Butch McLean could shoot, sit a horse, spin a yarn, track a varmint or villain, and pleasure a woman better than anyone alive. Butch's particular talents held little value for the new folks pouring into the Southwest like locusts to a barbecue, but the old-timers still appreciated and tolerated the likes of Butch McLean.

On that late night in April no one fussed much when Butch kicked open the swinging doors to Angel's Heaven on Earth, while holding a pistol in each hand, and called out, "I am here to rescue Miss Angel. Everyone out now or I will be forced to shoot you."

The five or so men still in the saloon left quickly, backs to the wall, watching Butch as they scurried out. Butch had been known to take potshots at more than just rabbits. Thirty seconds later, the room was clear, except for the smoke, and Angel came from around the bar, hands on her cinched waist, blond curls framing her face and tickling the top of her bosom.

Butch walked toward Angel, guns still in the air, and leaned over and kissed her pearly white neck, and then her breasts— one at a time.

"Don't be doin' that unless you mean it," Angel said.

"Darlin'," Butch said. "I always mean it. I don't have an insincere bone in my entire body."

"Dammit, Butch," Angel said. "Those were paying customers. Some day I'm gonna really be in trouble and nobody will believe it!"

"Just call me the cowboy who cried wolf," Butch said.

"Cow*girl*," Angel said.

"Aww, Angie," Butch said as she dropped the pistols onto the bar. "I was just trying to have some fun."

"Sometimes you are more of an asshole than any man I know," Angel said. "The law is gonna put you in jail if you keep doing this kind of thing. Just wait until I close up and you can sneak in the back like all my other girls do. Now I'm gonna let the boys back in." She started walking toward the door.

"Let me take a trip up your dress first," Butch said.

Angel laughed.

"I'll be glad to," she said. "After the boys finish their drinks. Now you can either stay here and be good or come back later and be bad." She opened the door and leaned outside. "Come on in, boys. She promises not to pistol-whip anybody."

Doc Broome stumbled in first, followed by Merle T. Connelly and Johnny Jack.

Butch sighed and turned back to the bar. This was not the ending to the night she had envisioned. Butch started to pick up her revolvers, but Angel slapped her hands down on them, pulled them away, and slipped them out of sight behind the bar.

"You can get them later," she said. "You know I don't allow weapons in my establishment."

"Well, then," Butch said, "I had better leave, since my body is a weapon. A weapon of love."

Hearing all this—since Butch did not understand the concept of a whisper—Johnny Jack and Merle laughed as they climbed back onto their bar stools.

Butch leaned close to Johnny Jack's right ear. "You remember, don't you, Jay Jay?"

Merle and Angel stopped and stared at Johnny Jack, whose dark skin was turning darker.

"He was a lot better lookin' back then," Butch said, "and I was a lot less particular."

With that, Butch staggered out of the bar. Or maybe she swaggered. It depended upon who you asked. Memories fog the truth, distort it, amplify it. Or expose it. But everyone appeared to be in good spirits, especially Butch, when she left Angel's Heaven on Earth. Rosey stood next to someone's automobile, her black and white coat nearly fluorescent in the moonlight. Her white tail swept across her black rump. Butch patted Rosey's almost all-white face. Black circled her left eye, and white spread across her neck, barrel, and flank and down her left rear leg like a kind of jagged almost horse-shaped white continent across the sea of black horse.

"I need to take a leak, Rosey. Then we'll be on our way. Or maybe not. Where's George? Have you seen George? Oh fer chrissakes, I'm talking to a horse's rear end." She giggled. "Not so much different than talking to a man."

Butch had come into town earlier with George, but he had business at the other end of this street a few blocks from the plaza. The nearly full moon lit up the ramshackle wooden buildings that seemed to lean one against the other. On the few occasions Butch actually noticed this particular bent to the buildings—

like now—she wondered what kept them up. "Whiskey, of course," Butch whispered. "We all need something to keep us standing."

She breathed deeply. A romp with Angel would have been fun, but this night air was bracing, nearly knocking the drunk off of her. She gazed up at the clear dark sky. The stars shivered and winked. She could hear the whisper of the *acequia madre* even though it was some distance away. She grinned. The full moon, silence, and alcohol made her senses preternatural. A chorus of coyotes began yipping at the moon. Someone was shouting out in the desert. Butch listened. Crazy Betty. Could be yelling at the coyotes or the moon. Or space aliens. Who knew? Her shouts died away.

The cottonwood trees across the street and down a bit stood tall and nearly bare in the moonlight, like tangled members of a Day of the Dead tableau, or a Danse Macabre. Despite this, the air smelled of spring the way only New Mexican air can: like dust, peppers, and the color blue.

Butch started to walk away from the buildings and into the night, forgetting why she was there, only wanting to get closer to the sound of the coyotes and the mother ditch. Suddenly the north sky lightened, and Butch looked up. A shooting star streaked across the sky. Butch laughed. If Crazy Betty saw that falling star she'd be full of space alien stories for days.

Butch heard a woman cry out in the darkness. Instantly she ran toward the sound, up over a silver rise and then down again. Running in the desert was plain stupid; running at night in the desert was a death wish. However, Butch could never resist the cry of a woman in trouble. And she was drunk.

Suddenly, she ran right into a person. They both fell back onto the ground. Butch jumped instantly to her feet. Nothing or no one was going to catch her on the ground: not a scorpion, rattler, or a man, certainly.

The body she knocked into was a bit slower getting up off the ground.

"Are you all right?" Butch asked. Butch always talked in a kind of drawl. Not Texan. Good Lord, no. Not Southern. Kind of Mexican, Native American, and plain American all rolled into one.

She reached her hand out. The man stood on his own, quickly dusting off his chaps with one arm; he kept the other arm bent at his side. He wore ammo belts crossed over his chest like a Mexican bandito; a cowboy hat shaded his face from Butch.

"You Pancho Villa or something?" Butch asked.

The man tried to step around her. Butch moved to block him.

"I heard a woman cry out," Butch said, noticing a black shape on the ground near a medium-sized paloverde whose yellow flowers looked bright white in the darkness. "That her?"

The man shook his head. "I was the one who yelled," he said, his English accented. Mexican. Clipped almost. From the upper class?

"I was thrown from my horse and was trying to get my bearings. I stumbled over that—that body. I yelled." He hesitated. "Like a woman. My voice . . . rises when I am . . . afraid."

"Happens to the best of us," Butch said. "I scream like a woman, too. Nothing wrong with that."

"But you are a woman," the man said.

"That's a fact," Butch said, "I am pleased to report."

She kept her eye on Bandito as she went toward the body. She squatted next to it. A man. She found his arm and felt for a pulse at his wrist.

"He's not dead," Butch said.

"Shit." The English word out of the man's mouth sounded desperate.

Butch stood and looked at Bandito.

"You wanna tell me something about this?"

"No," he said. "I don't know you. I don't know him."

Butch could see Bandito's arm now in the moonlight. Part of his sleeve was dark.

"He shot you?" Butch said. "I didn't hear a shot. Looks like you're bleeding kind of heavy."

"He shot me some time back," Bandito said quickly, as though relieved to speak of it. "He and his *compañero* have been tracking me. My ex-wife's husband won't let me have my son, Frederico. He's four years old. He needs his—he needs his father. I went to Mexico to get him back, and my ex-wife's husband sent his thugs after me after I made a . . . fuss."

Butch chuckled. "A fuss, eh? I kinda like making a fuss myself." Something about this young man tickled her. Like Angel's blond curls. "So there's two of them? Where's the other one?"

"I fell from my horse. And I found this man who was tracking me. I hit him with a rock from behind. I don't know where the other man is."

Butch tried to remember if she had seen any strangers at Angel's. The man on the ground moaned.

"Come on," Butch said to Bandito. "I guess I better get you outta here. The doc is drunker than I am, so I'll take you home. TomA and Trick will either cure you or kill ya."

"I'd prefer the cure," Bandito said.

"Wouldn't we all."

Butch and Bandito went over the rise and down again, toward Rosey. Butch untied the horse and got up into the saddle. She reached her arm down and helped the man up behind her.

"I'm Butch McLean, by the way," Butch said as she turned Rosey around. She gently kicked the horse into a gallop.

"I'm Mateo Cruz," the man said.

"Yeah, well, hang on, Bandito," Butch said. "We're gonna get out of Dodge."

A moment later, the darkness swallowed the trio.

Mateo Cruz's grip on Butch's waist began to weaken as they neared their destination. In the distance, Butch could see the soft glow of the lantern TomA had left outside the gate of Wayward Ranch, the former home of St. Anne's Home for Wayward Boys.

"We're almost there," Butch said, gripping Bandito's good arm that loosely held onto Butch's waist.

Butch reached for one of her pistols to shoot it off to let TomA or someone know that she needed help, and then she remembered she had left her pistols at Angel's.

Rosey trotted up to the closed wooden gate. Butch leaned over and grabbed the clapper of the bell and rang it.

Bandito slumped against Butch.

"Sorry, Bandito," Butch said. "You ain't my type. At least not tonight. I was in the mood for some Angel. But what the hell, put you in a dress and we'll see what we can work out."

The gate opened, and TomA and Patrick—Trick—were soon next to Rosey.

"Shot," Butch said as the two men reached up to pull the nearly unconscious man off the horse. "Doc was drunk."

The thin TomA hooked one of Bandito's arms around his neck, and Trick, who was slightly bigger, put the other arm around his neck. They half-carried and half-dragged Mateo Cruz toward the Big House.

Butch rode Rosey through the open gates, then jumped down, picked up the lantern TomA and Trick had left on the ground, then pulled the gate shut. She made certain the gate was closed tight, the latch in place. After all, it was her responsibility: She was the head of security at Wayward.

"Come, Rocinante," she said to the paint. "If I stall long enough I won't have to watch all the bloody bits."

The horse followed Butch away from the Big House, past

the casita, chapel, and bunkhouse to the corral. Butch set the lantern on top of a fence post. She could hear the horses chewing in the corral, saw their dark shapes under the moon. One horse let out a short whinny. Rosey answered it.

Butch undid the cinch strap and pulled the saddle and blanket off Rosey and set them just inside the barn.

"I'll take care of her." Hunter stepped out of the shadows.

"She's been ridden hard," Butch said. "She needs to walk it off."

"Whoa!" Hunter said as she came closer to Butch. "Smells like you need to walk it off, too." The girl waved her hand in front of her face.

"You need to have more respect for your elders, child," Butch said as she started to walk toward the Big House. "Or I'll tell you-know-who that you were out communin' with nature again."

"Go ahead," Hunter said. "Seventeen is old enough."

"Old enough for what?" Butch stopped and turned around. That didn't sound good.

"For everything," Hunter said. Her arm moved up and down as she curried the horse.

Butch walked back to Hunter and Rosey.

"What's goin' on?" Butch asked. "Something happen? I thought you were out doing the wild with Jimmy."

Hunter stopped and looked at Butch. "That's all I meant. TomA and Trick like Jimmy. You know that. So it would be all right to tell them."

Butch took the girl's chin in her hand and gently turned it toward the light. Her face was dirty, and she had a red spot over her left cheekbone.

"What happened? Did Jimmy hit you? I'll kill him." She reached for her guns. Still at Angel's. "Goddamn it."

"Jimmy wouldn't hurt me, Butch," Hunter said. "You know

that. I tripped. I was trying to get back to the house before . . . before they figured out I was gone, and I tripped and fell."

Butch squinted. "I've known you since you were born," she said. "I've always known when you were lying. Always."

Hunter looked at her. "So? Am I lying?"

They stared at each other for several seconds. Breathless.

"Oh hell," Butch said, letting out her breath. "I don't know. I was bluffin'. You sure you all right? Want Trick to look you over?"

"Geez, Butch. You're worse than an old woman. I tripped is all. I'm all right."

"Well, how about I go shoot Jimmy anyway? Your daddies would probably give me a raise. You're too young." She started to walk away again.

"How old were you?" Hunter asked.

"Jesus, girl. You want to have that discussion now? I've got a man in the house with a bullet hole in his arm."

"Yeah. So? I've known you since I was born, nearly. You hate the sight of blood."

"I don't so much hate it," Butch said. "I just don't want to get in the way while Patrick works his healing charms."

"You could bullshit the skin off a rattlesnake, but you can't bullshit me," Hunter said.

"Watch your mouth, girl," Butch said. "Awright. I'll tell you. When I was staying here, when it was still St. Anne's and my momma was long ago hanged and dead and Grandma Crow was dead and they brought me here, I had to learn to fend for myself to survive those nuns and those boys. I was ten and the boys were all . . . wayward."

"Horny as hell?"

"That, too. Before long I had to fight off their advances. That's how I learned to fight. I kicked, gouged, and cursed my way out of more than one encounter. Then Sister Jeanmarie—

she was Irish—came along and she showed me how to really fight. And how to shoot. She also kept me out of the dormitory and living with the nuns. Sometimes that sick fuck Sister Claw and Father Brufield had me inside the dormitory as a temptation for his boys to resist, he said. But that's another story."

"Yes, it is," Hunter said. "I asked about your first time having sex, not the first time someone tried to rape you. I know what you're doing. You're trying to scare me. But Jimmy doesn't scare me. He's very gentle."

"Oh Christ, sister. I do not want to talk about this."

"Since when? Your conquests are legendary."

"That's just bragging," Butch said, leaning against the fence. "But talking about the first time. Hmm." She shook her head. "The first time I was kissed proper was under that old cotton-wood in back of the chapel here. Her name was Suzanne. I was thirteen and she was about the same age, maybe a little older. She wanted to practice on me before she kissed her boyfriend. At least that's what she said. She was quite enthusiastic. That's all I'll say. Except that her lips were so soft. So soft. Like when your lips first touch a peach. That soft peach fuzz. Mmmmm. Suzanne."

"Butch, not your first kiss. Your first time having sex."

"That is a story for another night," she said. "Now walk that horse." Butch pushed away from the fence. "You sure you're all right?"

"I'm sure," Hunter said.

"You know you can always come to me," Butch said. "About anything. I'll help. I might make fun of you first. But I'll help you out eventually."

"Go away," Hunter said. "I hope that man's wound is really bloody. Gory. I hope you faint."

"Honey, I don't faint," she said. "How could a woman be a woman if she fainted every time she saw blood? Wouldn't that be inconvenient. And ain't that a terrible thing to wish on a man. A bloody wound." Butch slapped the girl on the butt. "See you later, kid."

Butch walked to the back of the Big House, ran up the short stack of steps, opened the thick wooden kitchen door, and went inside.

Mateo Cruz sat at the long wooden table, his left arm resting on the table while Trick wrapped it in gauze, a wash bowl with a bloody cloth swimming in hot water and a bottle of alcohol nearby. TomA sat by the huge kiva fireplace where a small fire snapped around green wood. On the other side of the room, Maria stood at a counter, spooning what looked like chicken verde onto two plates.

Cruz glanced at Butch, then looked quickly away.

"What are you doing here this late, darlin'?" Butch asked as she walked over to Maria and sat at a stool at the counter. Maria dropped a fork onto one of the plates, then pushed it across the counter to Butch.

"Satisfying your every whim," Maria said.

"Hardly," Butch said. She took a bite of the chicken verde. "You are a goddess, Maria. Javier at a card game?"

She nodded. "At our house. Let him wake up in the morning surrounded by their mess and clean it up. Not me. Have you seen Jimmy?"

Butch shook her head.

"You're lucky," Trick said to Bandito. "It's just a graze. A deep graze, but it'll heal. Probably have a scar and you might lose some muscle strength."

Butch looked over at them. In the golden light of the lamps and fire, Bandito looked even younger than Butch had first guessed. He still had cheek fuzz rather than stubble. Twenty? Twenty-five? Already with a kid and an ex-wife? And running for his life. He had a more complicated life than Butch's. Not that her life was really that complicated. Kind of routine actually, when she thought about it.

"Butch," TomA said, "please tell me you did not have anything to do with this."

"If I'd a shot him, he'd be dead," Butch said.

"Really?" TomA said. "Last I saw you target practicing, you couldn't hit a broad standing at the side of a barn, let alone a man in the dark."

Butch raised an eyebrow. "Normally I would shoot you for such blatant disrespect, but I left my pistols at the gates of heaven."

"Beneath Angel's skirts?"

"Something like that."

"Keep this wound clean," Trick said to Mateo. "I'll change the dressing tomorrow."

Maria took the other plate over to the table and put it in front of Mateo.

Trick patted Mateo's arm lightly, then picked up the wash basin and left the room.

"Where you come from, Mateo Cruz?" Maria asked in Spanish.

"Chihuahua," Cruz said.

"You are a long way from home," Maria continued in Spanish.

Butch and TomA glanced at each other. Had Maria forgotten they spoke Spanish too?

"As are you," Cruz said.

"I was born here," Maria said. "And I don't like strangers tracking blood to our door. Then all kinds of trouble starts sniffing around."

"Hey, Maria," Butch said. "You keep flirting with him, I'll be forced to tell Javier."

Maria looked over at Butch, seemingly startled. TomA got

up from the fire and sat at the table with Cruz. Maria went back to the counter.

"What's eating you?" Butch asked Maria quietly. "We have strangers showing up here every day."

It was that kind of place, a ranch but also a way station of sorts—or a sanctuary—where artists, misfits, and other lost souls came to sit for a spell. Or as TomA often put it, "Where queers have no fears."

Maria opened the door on the wooden stove and peered inside for a moment. Then she slammed it shut. It popped open. She shut it again, this time more carefully.

"Here," Butch said, pushing the plate toward her. "Why don't you eat some of your own cooking? It's mighty tasty."

Maria stared at her. Butch smiled and handed her the fork. The older woman took it and made a stab at the chicken and came up with a bite.

"Isn't that better?"

"Something is not right," Maria said. "I can feel it."

"It's only the full moon," Butch said.

Butch had known Maria since a group of white people had dropped Butch off at the front door of St. Anne's School for Wayward Boys. Sister Michael Joseph Tom Dick and Harry or whatever her name was—Butch thought of her as Sister Claw— had stood next to Butch as the white people in the wagon left them in the dust, her hand on Butch's shoulder, her fingers digging into her like a vise. Later that day after Sister Claw forced Butch to put on a dress, Butch ran away to the kitchen where Maria stood behind the counter slapping flat bread dough back and forth between her hands. Maria was probably twenty years old then, maybe younger.

"You are the new one," Maria had said. "You must be hungry."

Butch had pulled out a wooden chair and sat at the table. A

few minutes later, Maria set a plate of blue corn tortillas, spotted beans, and squash in front of her.

"Don't tell the Father or Mother," Maria said. "They think the blue corn is poison. Of course they think anything to do with the Indians is poison. What's your name?"

"Butch," she said.

Maria went back to making flat bread at the counter. "Your mother named you Butch? Did the women bless you with corn pollen at dawn as the sun came up?"

"My mother was white," Butch said. "And a whore. She killed herself when I was a baby. I've eaten food like this at the Pueblo with my grandma."

"Some day you should have the blessing," Maria said. "I can make you another plate if you're still hungry, Butch."

"Her name is not Butch." Sister Claw came into the kitchen then, her hands hidden within the folds of her habit. "She won't tell me her true name. I have consulted with Father Brufield, and we have agreed we will call you Mary until we find out what your Christian name is."

"I am not a Christian," Butch said, "and my name is not Mary."

Sister Claw's hand came out of cloth, slapped Butch across the face, and withdrew into the fabric once again so quickly that Butch thought she had imagined it—until her face began pulsing with the red mark Sister Claw's hand had left behind.

"Sister Michael Joseph!" Maria said.

"My hand is an extension of God's love," Sister Claw said. "She has been living as a heathen long enough. It's time she became civilized, like all the boys here. It is our duty and responsibility."

Sister Claw turned and left the room. Butch listened to the whisper of the cloth as she went and knew she should memorize that sound, become alert to it.

Maria said, "They're not all like her. And she doesn't mean to be so heartless. It's just that she was born without one."

Butch smiled and finished her meal. She took the dress off soon after that. She walked about the place in her underwear. The boys laughed and pointed. Sister Claw and Father Brufield beat the crap out of her. She persisted. Every time they put a dress on her, she took it off, ripped it to shreds, and walked around in her undergarments. Then they whipped her. Finally one of the nuns suggested a compromise: Butch could wear pants except when she went to church. Then she had to put on a dress. She agreed, and the beatings stopped. For the most part. And the kitchen—with Maria in it—became Butch's sanctuary.

Now Trick returned to the kitchen. "It's time for bed," he said. "TomA, you've been up since before dawn."

"Painting, love," TomA said. "It's not like I was working." He grinned, stood, and stretched. Trick took one of TomA's hands in his and kissed the top of it.

"You are welcome to stay as long as you like," TomA said to Cruz, "although we're going to have to put you up in the attic. We're expecting a full house after the ditch cleaning for the Wayward Art Spectacle. You're welcome to stay for that."

Butch groaned.

The three men looked at her.

"Nothing more boring than listening to a bunch of men discuss art. Women, yes, maybe. Then at least there'd be something beautiful to look at."

"Women come, too," TomA said. "Don't listen to her. It's quite stimulating. She loves it."

"By the way," Trick said, "Jezebel might be back in the area."

"What?" Butch said.

"Javier heard it from one of the men at the card game," Maria said. "A couple of calves were taken from the Foster ranch."

Butch shook her head. "Naw. Just some tourist or Easterner who doesn't know the difference between an Appaloosa and a jaguar."

"Anyway," Trick said. "Could you check it out? She does have a habit of showing up where you are."

"Not true," Butch said. "Whoever told you that is a liar."

"You told us," Trick said.

"See what I mean?"

"Take Mr. Cruz up to his room, will you?" TomA said. "I am a bit tired and those stairs are hard on my knees. Put him in the one at the west end. The door to the other room sticks. If you see Hunter, please tell her to get to bed."

Trick put his arm across TomA's shoulders, and they left the room. TomA appeared to be limping a bit. Butch started to say something and then stopped. Hunter was right; she was acting like a worried old lady.

"You ready, Bandito?"

Cruz stood. "That was very good, Señora Maria. Thank you."

"Why do you need all those bullets?" Maria asked. "You look like you are dressed for a war."

"It is just the style where I come from," Cruz said.

"The style of bandits, you mean," Maria said. "We don't allow guns in this house."

Cruz glanced at Butch.

"Hey, don't look at me," she said. "I left my guns in town. Some uppity woman took them from me."

"As you can see," Cruz said, "I have no guns, only bullets. The guns were in my saddlebags."

Maria picked up the dish from the table. "Drink that tea," Maria said. "You think I made it for my health? No. It's for yours. It will help with the pain."

Cruz picked up the cup and gulped the tea. Then he set the

cup back on the table. Maria picked it up and went back to the sink.

"I'll show you your room," Butch said, and she led the man out of the kitchen and down the long hallway.

"I don't suppose there's any way of going back and finding my horse?" Cruz asked as they walked into the Big Room.

"What kind of horse is it?" Butch asked. "I'll put the word out in the morning." She picked up the lamp on the low table next to the leather sofa.

"An Appaloosa I—I found," he said.

They climbed a set of stairs that led to the second floor.

"A gelding, stallion, mare?"

Cruz frowned. "I don't really know."

What kind of person didn't know what kind of animal they were riding?

"You are a strange bird," Butch said.

They walked down a long narrow hallway and then up a short stairway to the upper floor. Every time Butch came up to these rooms she thought about Sister Claw and Father Brufield. They locked her up here—in the punishment room—after her beatings because they knew she could not bear being kept indoors in such a small space.

They never found out that she had quickly figured out how to escape her prison and wander freely through the nearly empty house.

Butch shook her head. That was ancient history, and she was not one of those whiners who spent time ruminating about her past.

"If your horse is a stallion, he's probably gone to find a mare," Butch said. "If it's a mare, she's probably looking for food and water. Gelding might stay right where he dropped you."

"He didn't drop me," he said. "I fell. I'm not a true horseman."

"Honestly? I wouldn't have guessed," Butch said. Her sarcasm was lost on the bandito.

The light from the lamp barely made a dent in the close stuffy darkness of the top floor. Butch walked down the hall without a glance toward the punishment room and opened the door to the other room. The lamp illuminated a small bed and tiny dresser. Butch set the lamp on the dresser and went to the window. It looked out over the silvery desert. She pushed the window open.

"There's a little night air for ya," Butch said.

Butch heard a scraping sound. She looked toward the open door.

"What was that?" she asked.

Cruz shrugged. "Sounded like it was close by."

They walked out into the narrow hall. Butch went to the punishment room door, turned the handle, and pushed on the door. It wouldn't open. She couldn't tell if it was locked or stuck, like TomA had said. She stood still for a moment and listened.

"Maybe a rat or squirrel," Butch said as she walked back to Cruz's room.

"Or a madwoman in the attic," Cruz said.

"What's that?"

"Have you ever read *Jane Eyre?*" Cruz asked.

"As a matter of fact," Butch said, "I have not. That been translated into Spanish?"

"I read it in English," he said.

"Do tell?" Butch could speak and understand Spanish fluently, but she could barely read it.

"Jane Eyre is a governess to a rich older man's charge," Cruz said. "They live in a mansion and sometimes when she's on the upper floors, Jane hears strange noises. She falls in love with the man, Rochester, and he with her. On their wedding day, just as she is about to say her vows, a man stops the wedding and declares Rochester is already married. His first wife is insane, and Rochester has her locked in the attic."

"Sounds like a good story," Butch said. "Especially if Jane rescues the first wife in the attic, and they run off together."

Cruz laughed. "That is not quite what happens. Jane does leave the man. The wife gets loose and burns down the mansion, crippling and blinding the man. Jane Eyre returns then, and they live happily ever after."

"Happily ever after?" Butch shook her head. "I like my version better."

"I think I might, too," he said. "Although when I was younger I felt sorry for the man. Now I am not quite so sympathetic."

Butch's mother's name was Jane. Maybe she had run afoul of her own Rochester. Only she hadn't made it out alive.

Outside the dog began barking.

"I better go see what's bothering Archie," Butch said. "When he was young, he'd bark at anything. Now that he's old, he doesn't usually bark at anything."

"Thank you for all you have done for me," Cruz said. "I appreciate it."

"Any time," Butch said. She glanced at Cruz, smiled uncomfortably, then hurried down the dark hall and stairs. He had a nice looking face, this Cruz fellah, and—quite frankly—a nice ass. She had not been attracted to an ass of that persuasion since she saw George coming out of the water a few years ago, his long black hair touching the top of his backside, and she had gasped at his beauty and had been glad (once again) that she was not a male and could easily hide her desire. She had been uncomfortable around him for many days afterward. Until he belched. Or farted. Or something. And she stopped lusting after him. He was just a guy. Sometimes she wished she was more attracted to more men more often. It would be easier. Women were a pain in the ass. Too much courting required. Which was probably why she had taken up with Johnny Jack for a short time a long while ago. And she had crossed to the other side on a few other occasions.

Why was she even thinking about this? Still drunk. Still unsatisfied. Angel had invited her to come back later. Maybe now was later.

She walked through the kitchen. Maria was gone. Archie still barked. Butch reached for her guns.

"Goddamn it!" she said when she realized they were still gone.

She stepped out the back door into darkness. Suddenly George was there beside her, carrying a lamp and a rifle. He tossed Butch the rifle and pulled out his pistol from its holster.

"Heard Jezebel is back in the area," George said. "Where'd you go anyway? I was looking for you in town."

"Long story," she said. "I'll believe Jezebel is back when I see her."

They walked toward the chicken house which was not far from the Big House. Butch heard the kitchen door open. She turned. Hunter stood on the steps.

"Don't shoot it if it's a coyote," Hunter shouted as Butch and George walked toward the coop that was near the backside of the house. "Or a mountain lion!"

"We promise to give whatever it is a stern warning, darlin'," Butch said.

As they got closer to the chicken house, Butch could hear the chickens squawking.

"Archie!" George called to the dog. "What do you see?"

The dog ran up to George, wagging his tail. George and Butch walked around to the front of the chicken house. Archie loped away to Hunter. The door to the chicken house was open.

George took the lantern and looked inside. The chickens chuck-chucked at him. "Nothing dead." He counted. "But one is missing. Isn't this door supposed to be latched?"

"At night," Butch said. Even so, they had a tall fence around the back to keep the critters away from the vegetable garden and the chickens. Butch squatted on the ground and looked for prints.

"I smell cat," George said as he stepped out of the chicken house and closed the door.

"Is this your Indian seventh sense or something? I thought you told me all that mystic stuff was bullshit."

"You can't smell anything because you've got the stink on you," George said.

"But cat?" Butch said, standing. "A lot of trouble for a mouthful."

They walked a bit until they were looking up at the branches of a cottonwood tree leaning over the fence. A coyote wouldn't climb a tree, but a mountain lion would. They had never had trouble from a mountain lion. Not this close to the house, not in April.

"Could be Jezebel," George said. "You know what they say."

"I don't know who the fuck *they* are," Butch said, "but they're wrong. Animals don't visit revenge upon people. People are the only ones who do that kind of shit."

"I'm with you on that, Butch," George said as they stood staring at the cottonwood in the darkness, "but you did kill one of her cubs."

"I don't believe I did," Butch said. "Goddamn it."

George laughed. "All right, we'll ignore the evidence for a minute. Maybe she wants you to hunt down the real killer and bring him to justice."

"You assume the killer is a he? Women can be as cruel as men."

"Witness you with your lovers."

"I am not cruel. I'm—"

"Inattentive? Indifferent? Inaccessible?"

"Jesus, George. I've got a hangover and I'm still drunk. Now you're ragging on me about how I treat women. What's your problem?"

"Just secretly in love with you, I guess," he said, "and wish you'd treat me so bad."

Butch looked over at him. He laughed.

"Nothing else we can do right now," he said. "Call it a night? I got some coffee on the stove in the casita."

They turned and walked back toward the Big House.

"Hey, I found this amazing-looking Appaloosa wandering around in the desert near Angel's," George said. "I tied it up near the saloon, but I'm hoping the owner doesn't show up. I was going to go back in the morning and get it."

"I know who owns it," Butch said. "He's here. Some guy shot him. Bandito. Er, Mateo Cruz. He claims his ex-wife's new husband sent some goons after him. Sounds pretty strange since he looks about two years old. Not old enough to have an ex-wife and a kid. I found one of the guys he said was following him. He had knocked him out with a rock. He thought he'd killed him, but he hadn't. The guy will wake up with a bad headache. I told Bandito I'd try to find his horse. He seems . . . a bit lost. I think I'll ride in and get the horse now." Maybe she could make a quick stop at Angie's on the way back. "You wanna come? I need to stop by Angie's and pick up my guns anyway."

"Yeah, right," George said. "I'm not sitting on my horse waiting for you all night again."

"No chance of that," Butch said. "The night is just about over."

The Appaloosa was still standing in front of Angel's, tied to the post. Butch and George got off their horses and looked at the pony. No one else was about. No lights. No sounds.

"I'll go in and get my pistols," Butch said.

"I'll take the pony and start back to the ranch," George said.

"You'll miss my great wit on the way home if you leave without me. You know you will."

Butch tried the saloon door, but it was locked. She went around the back and tried the door that led to Angel's apartment. It opened easily. Butch smiled. At last. She could almost feel Angel's skin against hers. Could imagine falling to sleep in her arms on her bed—which was much more comfortable than Butch's raggedy ass bed in the casita. She was about to shout her arrival when it occurred to her Angel might be asleep. She would be considerate and keep her voice down. And then she'd tell Angel how considerate she'd been when she woke her up to make love to her.

Butch walked softly down the hall to the bedroom. The door was open, and she could see by the lantern light that Angel was in bed.

And Merle T. Connelly was on top of her.

"Oh shit, Angie," Butch said, standing in the doorway.

"Butch!" Angel said, pulling up the covers as Merle climbed off her and sat next to her, shaking his head.

"I've seen you naked, sugar," Butch said. "No sense covering up now. Merle T. Connelly? That's disgusting."

"Don't shoot me, Butch," he said.

Butch reached for her guns. "Goddamn it. I gotta get those things back. I ain't gonna shoot you. Angie, I knew you had other lovers. But this one? He's got a dick."

"He's not a dick!"

"I said he has a dick, Angel," Butch said.

"So do you!" she said. "You just can't see yours. Except when you're waving around those pistols."

"Let's not get insulting," Butch said, "so we can end this peacefully."

Butch turned away and walked toward the door that opened into the saloon. Why did it have to be Merle T. Connelly? Something about him always got on her nerves. He reminded her too much of the boys at St. Anne's Home for Wayward Boys, especially the ones who were always trying to start a fight and then blaming her when the nuns came running. And as far as Butch could tell, Connelly didn't work for a living; he lived off his daddy's income.

A moment later, she heard Angel's bare feet on the floor behind her.

"He wants to get married," Angel said. "And have children. He's stable. He's constant. Goddamn it, Butch. Look at me."

Butch stopped and turned to face Angel in the dark. They stared at each other.

"Well, don't you have anything to say?" Angel asked.

"I'll miss you, darlin'," Butch said, "and I wish you all the best. Now I'm gonna get my . . . cold hard guns and go on home."

She turned and pushed the door open and stepped into the saloon. It still smelled of beer and smoke. She had the room memorized. Even in the dark she could easily walk to the break in the bar and reach around for her guns. Which she did.

Then, without a backward glance, she went to the front door, unlocked it, and went through it to where George was getting on his horse. He held the reins of the Appaloosa in one hand and the reins of his horse in the other.

"That was quick," George said. "Even for you."

Butch didn't say anything. She got back on Rosey.

They headed away from town. The night was graying into morning. Some warbler began to sing, but Butch could not quite place it. Her drunk was now almost completely gone.

What a waste of whiskey the night had been.

They traveled in silence as the gray night turned to gold green day. The sky became that perfect blue Butch had never seen any other place except in a New Mexican sky.

"George," Butch said, "did you ever wonder where the hell your life is going?"

"No," he said. "And neither do you. You need to listen to the dawn."

"I've got a hangover, and I haven't even slept yet."

"Some corn pollen crushed on your forehead," he said. "A prayer to the directions. A dip in the water. You'd come to your senses."

For a moment, Butch imagined herself next to the water, beside Sacred Lake, naked, awaiting the dawn, awaiting the plunge into the icy water.

"Things are changing," Butch said. "I can feel it. And you know that's sayin' something because I don't feel nothing." She laughed. George was silent.

"I found Angel in bed with Merle T. Connelly," Butch said.

"That could not have been an attractive picture," George said.

Butch laughed. "That's putting it mildly. She was mad at me. I don't think I understand women, George. At all."

"I don't know what to say to that, Butch."

Butch heard an automobile horn behind her.

Deputy Martin Paper drove up next to them. They reined the horses to a stop.

"You hear?" Martin asked.

"Hear what?" Butch said. "It's the butt crack of dawn. All I hear are the birds and the ringing in my ears."

"Found a dead man just over the hill," Martin said, pointing behind him, out the window. "Sheriff's over there right now. Told me to go look for anything suspicious. The man was shot through the heart. Or the liver. Heart's in the middle, right? Or is that the stomach? Anyway, they're already talking about re-naming that place Dead Man Gulch. Has quite a ring, doesn't it? And won't that be ironic? I mean finding a dead man there."

Butch and George looked at each other.

"Who exactly did you fuck to get that badge?" Butch asked.

"Gotta go," Martin said. "Nice Appaloosa."

He drove away. Butch pulled her neckerchief up around her nose and mouth.

"Those things stink," she said. "Should be a law against them."

"I suppose that dead man is your unconscious man," George said.

"I suppose he is."

Two

Butch heard George singing in the other room when she opened her eyes. She lay still for a moment. The song reminded her of the time they had lived in Grandma Crow's place after Butch was run off St. Anne's Home for Wayward Boys. She'd walked back toward Pueblo land, even though she hadn't been certain where she was when the nuns closed the gate behind her.

She had smelled Sacred Lake and walked toward it. Or maybe she had heard Grandma Crow calling to her. By the time she reached Grandma Crow's old place, her feet were torn and bloody. Her old shoes hadn't stood up to the desert treasures she had to traverse to find her way back home.

She had walked toward the dilapidated structure that was Grandma Crow's home. She was only fifteen years old, ready to slouch into the ground and disappear like the old adobe house.

Then George came out of the house. He hadn't been much older than she was. Living away from the pueblo and his people. He took her satchel and tried to take the tatters box she held firmly against her body—the one with her mother's things in it. She wouldn't let him have it. She never let anyone touch it.

Not even Grandma Crow. But she had gone into the house with him. He had cleaned her feet, dressed her wounds, fed her. They probably became best friends for life in those first few moments together.

She knew nothing about him then. He knew her. Even before she told him her story, which she did, eventually, one day as they watched the sun fall into the desert.

She couldn't tell him much about her mother because Butch didn't know much, only what Grandma Crow or Grandma No One had told her. Grandma Crow wasn't her real grandmother. She was the old Pueblo woman who happened to be walking through the desert when she found Butch's mother hanging from an old cottonwood growing close to the river, so close most people standing in that spot wouldn't have been able to tell the difference between the song the wind made through the cottonwood leaves and the song the water made over the river-bed. She also found Butch.

The People called the old Pueblo woman Grandma No One. The Other People called her Crow Woman. Or maybe it was the other way around. Butch called the old woman Grandma Crow. She had another name, too, but Butch didn't hear it often. She was only ten when Grandma Crow died, so she didn't remember the other name any more. Except sometimes she heard the Wind whisper it. Or a Magpie would call it out. Then she would remember.

The Other People called her Crow Woman because they believed she collected shiny things, like crows did. Only everyone knew crows didn't really collect shiny things, at least not the crows in this desert. Crows only picked up things they could eat or weave into their nests. Grandma Crow picked up Butch. She didn't eat her, so Butch supposed she brought her home to weave her into her nest. Make her part of her home.

From as far back as Butch could remember, Grandma No

One told her that her mother was a whore, a word Butch didn't know. When she learned that meant her mother took money from men to have sex, Butch didn't understand why people thought that was a bad thing. "We all got to make a living," she said. She said this to the sky. To the horses. To the coyotes. Later she said it to George.

Besides, Grandma No One lied about everything. Or nearly. She told Butch her mother's name was Jane Sarah McLean. Butch believed that was true because Grandma Crow gave Butch the box she had found near her mother's hanging body, near Butch herself, who was an infant at the time. Or a toddler. Her age changed with the telling. It was a small box, made out of tin, with keepsakes from her mother's life. On the top of the box, someone—her mother?—had painted the word "tatters." So Butch called it her tatters box. Sometimes she called it her tattered box, or her tattered treasure chest.

Inside the box were a couple of letters addressed to Jane (and sometimes to Sarah), a small cameo with the letter "B" carved into it—the letter "B" with a flower blooming from the last flourish—a whistle, and other odds and ends. Over the years, Butch had added a thing or two herself.

When Butch was a girl hiding from Grandma No One, she would spend hours looking at the things her mother had left behind in that tin box. She imagined sitting by the river with her mother, under the shade of the old cottonwood trees. Her mother would tell Butch what each and every thing in the box meant to her.

"The 'B' is for beautiful and it was carved the day you were born," she'd say. Or "My daddy, your grandfather, gave me this whistle when I was a girl so I could always whistle for my friends. I saved it to pass onto you." (Later when Butch was at St. Anne's Home for Wayward Boys, she would imagine her mother giving her advice on how to beat the boys bloody. And then she'd tell Butch how to burn down the home without getting caught.)

Butch would pick through the tin until Grandma No One became Grandma Crow again and the two of them would go out into the desert or to the riverside and listen for the truth.

Grandma Crow said the Wind always told the truth, no matter what direction it came from. "That's where you go for answers," she told Butch. And if you couldn't understand the Wind, ask Eagle to translate. Or Cottonwood. Or Rattlesnake. Only stand far back from Rattlesnake. He was related to Grandma No One and could strike out at you, even as he was telling the truth.

Butch never complained about having a bad childhood. She never even thought about things like that. She grew up, like other people did. She was sorry her mother thought she had to kill herself. She was glad Grandma Crow had taken her in. She shuddered to think what would have happened if some holy roller had found her and dressed her in petticoats and taken her to church every Sunday.

No, Grandma Crow was meant for her. She only wished Grandma Crow had given Butch her mother's suicide note before she died. Butch knew there was one. Unless Grandma Crow had lied about that, too. Grandma Crow had sworn she would give the note to Butch when she was old enough. Butch often asked, "Old enough for what?" Grandma Crow never answered. Butch knew better than to ask Grandma No One about it. Grandma Crow said she'd hidden the note and it was no good looking for it because it would be invisible to Butch until Grandma Crow decided it was time. Or until Butch was ready.

Butch didn't ruminate on the fact that Grandma Crow had died without revealing where the note was. She figured she would find it eventually. She had asked the East Wind about it once and it had told her the note would become visible to her one day. And Butch knew the Wind always told the truth.

Now Butch threw off a thin blanket and turned over in bed. Next to the bed, on a stool George had made for her, was the tatters box.

Why was she thinking about all this old stuff today?

Who cared? None of it mattered.

Not really.

"Hey," George called from the other room. "Get your lazy drunk ass self out of bed. We've got work to do."

"Shut up!"

George came into the room.

"Have some respect," Butch said. "I ain't dressed yet."

George rolled his eyes. "I've seen your dirty long johns a million times," he said. "Sheriff heard you were wandering around in the dark last night. Wants you to come in and look at the body. See if you recognize him."

Butch sat up, put her feet on the cold floor, and rubbed her face.

"I'm getting too old for this shit," she said. "Maybe it's time—"

"To stop drinkin' so much?" George asked. "Time to stop staying up all night whorin'? Time to take a look at your life and get your shit together?"

Butch looked up at George. She wondered if her eyes were as bloodshot as George's. Naw. Probably worse. George did not drink like she did. Hardly drank at all, actually. Was partial to lemonade.

"I was gonna say I think maybe it's time to get something to eat. You make me breakfast yet?"

"Breakfast?" George said. "It's almost supper time." He kicked the bed. "Come on now."

"Go away," Butch said.

She got up, pushed George out of the room, and slammed

the door shut. She looked at the basin of cold water on the dresser. "It's now or never," she said. She plunged her hands into the water and then splashed her face, neck, under her arms and breasts.

She took some clothes off and put on others. She ran her fingers through her hair and then stepped out of the room and into the kitchen area.

"Mateo Cruz is up and around," George said. "Wants to leave. TomA is trying to talk him out of it."

George and Butch walked into the blue blue day together. Butch saw Hunter and Jimmy by the corrals, their heads together. They looked up when George and Butch came out of the casita. Hunter waved. Butch nodded.

"Notice lately that those two seem to be up to something all the time?" Butch said.

George shrugged. "They're teenagers. What do you expect?"

"Unswerving loyalty and worship," Butch said. "Nothing less."

"Dream on," George said.

"And tequila," Butch added. "I expect tequila."

Butch sprinted up the steps, opened the back door, and went inside the main house.

Mateo Cruz sat at the long table in the kitchen. Trick and TomA sat opposite him. Maria stood over the stove, cooking up something. They all looked over at Butch and George as they came into the house

Mateo Cruz smiled, and Butch's stomach did a flip-flop.

"Wow," Butch said. Mateo's eyes were dark brown, his long straight hair was blacker than a raven's, and a light fuzz covered his cheeks and upper lips. He was beautiful.

"What's this 'wow'?" Maria asked. "'Wow' that you finally got up and got dressed? Or 'wow' that you were up all night carousing. Sit down and I'll feed your lazy ass. George, you want something?"

"I'm good," George said. He sat next to Mateo.

"I was thinking how fucking gorgeous he is," Butch said. "I hadn't noticed in the dark. What are you, twenty?"

Mateo's face turned red.

Butch sat across from him, next to Trick.

Maria brought over a plate of scrambled eggs and tortillas and dropped it in front of Butch. "If you're waiting for one of us to apologize for her," Maria said, "you'll be here all day. Butch says what everyone is thinking."

"I—I'm twenty-seven," Mateo said. His voice was squeaky, as though he was frightened. He cleared his throat. "I was always the runt of my father's litter."

"Your father's?" Maria said. "Hmph. What did he have to do with it? Your mother birthed that litter. You men think you're the center of the universe. Hah! You couldn't do nothing without us. You wouldn't even exist without us."

Trick groaned. "That is our cue to leave," he said. "We have lots to do to prepare for the Wayward Art Spectacle."

"Butch," TomA said as he got up from the table. "Mr. Cruz wants to leave us. I think he should tell you his story. Trick and I don't need to know the details. But Butch can help you out, Mateo. She's one of the good guys. She's a problem solver. And if someone is trying to harm you, they'd never find you here. If they did, George and Butch would keep them away from you."

"How's security looking for the Spectacle?" Trick asked.

"It'll be fine," Butch said. "As always. I saw that war veteran hanging around a few days ago, but I chased him away."

"War veteran?" TomA asked.

"The Hermit," Butch said.

TomA looked at Patrick. Patrick said, "Herman Peterson. He got back from the war a few months ago, was staying at the

McLoughlin Boarding House. He was looking for work."

"Can't we help him out?" TomA asked.

"I don't trust him," Butch said. "He's got shell shock or soldier's heart or whatever they call it. He could be dangerous."

"You don't trust anyone," George said.

"And neither do you," Butch said. She ate a mouthful of eggs. "I've seen him. He's got that stare. I don't like it."

"Well, it's up to you," TomA said. "I trust your instincts, but part of the reason we're here is to help people like that. Remember what you were like when I found you outside the gates."

"Drunk and ready to burn the place down," Butch said. "You should have never let me in. Look what's happened. You can't get rid of me to save your life."

TomA and Trick smiled at her, and then they left the kitchen. Butch glanced at Mateo, who was watching her. God, he was about the prettiest man she had ever seen. She glanced at George. He rolled his eyes, got up, and went over to Maria and got a cup of coffee. They talked quietly with one another.

"Well," Butch said, "what do you wanna tell me? I may think you're cute, but I'll run you off, too, if I think you might cause this place or any of these people to come to harm."

Mateo shook his head. "I intend no harm," he said. "I am prepared to leave this morning."

Butch put her hand up. "Hold on," she said. "Tell me your sad story."

"Only if you tell me yours first," Mateo said. He smiled slightly.

George laughed loudly. Too loudly. Butch glanced back at him.

"Come on," George said. "He's flirting with you. It's a waste of time, Cruz. She only likes tall, dark, and womanly."

"Not true," Butch said quickly. A little too quickly. "I always say I don't discriminate because of gender."

She grinned at Mateo, who blushed again.

"This is too difficult to watch," Maria said. "Get out of my kitchen, all of you."

"Hold your horses," Butch said. "I haven't finished."

The kitchen got quiet. Butch grimaced and looked over at Maria.

"I apologize," Butch said. "I know this is your space and your place and I'm only a visitor. Could we stay a few more minutes? It won't be long."

"You may stay," Maria said as she grabbed a basket. "Only because I need to go out to the garden."

George made a face at Butch and followed Maria out of the kitchen.

"Don't know what's wrong with those two," Butch said. "You were saying last night that your ex-wife was after you. I'm confused by that. Is divorce even legal in Mexico?"

"As of last year it is," he said. "I didn't want the divorce. My wife cheated on me. She got remarried, but she died recently. My son should be with me. Her husband is rich and powerful. He won't let me see young Frederico. So I tried to take him, sneak him from the hacienda. They accused me of kidnapping. I had to run for my life. They know I will never give up until I have my son, so they've come after me here."

"That's quite a story," Butch said.

Mateo Cruz looked directly into Butch's eyes. "I would do anything to get my son back."

"I understand," Butch said. She cleared her throat. Nothing pissed her off more than powerful rich people trying to put the screw on someone.

Actually, nothing pissed her off more than powerful rich people period. Didn't have to do nothing but exist.

She knew she would help Mateo Cruz. But she had to get the lay of the land.

"They found a dead guy in the desert last night," Butch said. "Near where I found you. You kill him?"

"I hit that man with a rock," Cruz said. "But he was alive when you checked him."

"This man they found was shot," Butch said.

Cruz shook his head. "I don't have any guns," he said.

"You had enough bullets on your bandolier for an army," Butch said.

"And if you check, you'll see that all the ammunition is still there," Cruz said. "I'm embarrassed to say I lost my gun some days ago."

"I will check it," Butch said. She was always careful—even when she was smitten. Her eyes widened at the thought. She was not *smitten.* Cruz was years younger than Butch and almost looked like a boy. Might be lying about his age. And Butch could not—would not—be smitten with a boy. She hadn't even been smitten with a boy when she was a girl. Well, there had been that one boy. No, she had been smitten with his sister Suzanne. Not him. She rubbed her eyes. She did not want to think about the boy or his Boston Brahmin mother.

"Are you all right?" Cruz asked.

"What?" Butch looked at him. "Oh, just thinking about old times for some reason this morning, like some old man sittin' on a rocker on his front porch. Must be too much drink." Butch grinned. "Or not enough." She cleared her throat. "I'll go into town and see what's up. You stay here. And I mean stay here on this ranch. You want me to trust you? That's the first thing you've got to do."

Mateo nodded. "To be honest, I feel like I could sleep for a few weeks. Except, have you ever slept up there?"

"Lots of times, when I was a kid. Not in your room, but the one down the hall."

"Did you ever hear any strange noises?"

"That was so long ago," Butch said. She wouldn't admit to it, but she remembered it all very clearly. She had heard noises when they first locked her in the room. For a while, she thought Grandma Crow was haunting her or the house. But she didn't let it get to her. She wasn't going to let any of the people of St. Anne's get to her. So she had escaped and wandered the house half the night until the nuns came up to get her in the morning. By then she had locked herself back into the room.

Once they left her in the room for three days with no food and only a bit of water. In one of their many attempts to break her. She had just smiled at them when they opened the door.

This probably contributed to their belief that she was the devil's spawn.

They never found out about the key she had secreted in the room. The key Maria had smuggled to her the first time she was locked in the room.

"Why did you ask about noises?" Butch asked. "Did you hear something last night?"

Mateo nodded. "Sounded like someone crying or muffled screams. I looked out the window and didn't see anything, but it sounded like it was coming from inside the house. I will admit I was still feeling knocked out from the gunshot wound and I did not get up to investigate."

"Maria's tea, I'm sure," Butch said. "I bet you wouldn't hear a thing now if you went up. Or you could sleep outside under the cottonwoods. Odds are no scorpion or rattlesnake will crawl up your leg."

"I'm not a gambling man," Cruz said. "I'll sleep upstairs."

Butch nodded. "We'll talk more later," she said.

They got up from the table and went in different directions. Butch glanced back at Cruz as he walked away.

Nice backside.

Butch shook her head and went outside. She could see Maria out in the fenced gardens, bending over something green. George was in the corral, trying to settle down one of the new colts, Lightning Bolt. George was good with most any horse but this new one—nicknamed Bolt—had him stumped. Hunter and Jimmy stood outside the stables, saddling Rosey and Bucket, George's horse.

"That's what I like to see," Butch said. "Children doing my work for me."

"We're not children," Hunter said. "We are young adults."

"Old young adults," Jimmy said.

Butch looked at Maria's son Jimmy. He looked like both of his parents, so he was a handsome kid. But he had his father's sense of humor. Not exactly witty.

"In any case," Butch said. She patted Rosey's rump. "Good morning, Rosey, my love."

Hunter turned her head slightly and Butch got a good look at her face. Her left eye sported a shiner.

"How'd you get that again?" Butch asked.

"I slipped and fell," she said.

Butch looked at Jimmy.

Jimmy made a noise. "She told me you asked if I did that. I can't believe you'd think I'd ever hurt her. I should tell my mother."

Butch rolled her eyes. "I'm already in the dog house with her. Don't you say a word or I'll give you a shiner."

Jimmy laughed.

"What's so funny?" Butch asked.

"Nothin'," he said. "I was imagining my father kickin' your ass."

Butch held up her fist. Jimmy stepped back.

"Your father could not kick Butch's ass," Hunter said. "Come on. Now your mom, that's another matter."

"Nobody is kicking anyone's ass," Butch said. "Sheesh.

What are you two up to anyway?"

"Just trying to help out," Hunter said. She grinned.

Butch laughed. She had been a sucker for Hunter since the first moment she'd seen her, some seventeen years earlier when she'd first come to Wayward Ranch when Hunter was only a few months old.

At the time, TomA had told Butch he had adopted Hunter from a prostitute who didn't want her. Later Butch heard rumors that Hunter was actually Trick's daughter. He had gotten drunk at Angel's one night and hit the sheets with one of the town's prostitutes. Butch had never judged Trick because of that. She had had her own rendezvous with the occasional prostitute. The woman Trick had been with apparently got pregnant and either died in childbirth or had the baby and left her with Trick on her way out of town.

Butch had always been suspicious of all the stories about Hunter's birth and parentage. For one thing, how would a prostitute know the child was Trick's? Unless Trick had a more than passing relationship with her, which seemed unlikely. Butch never asked. It was none of her business. Her own mother was a prostitute. Didn't matter. She only knew that Trick's and TomA's relationship had been strained when she first came to Wayward. And then it wasn't. TomA fell in love with Hunter, so it soon didn't matter how she happened to be created.

"Tell me why you're trying to butter me up," Butch said.

"I've been watching George with that colt," Hunter said. "Doesn't look like he's getting far. You know, Herman Peterson is good with horses. I heard he can sing his way into any horse's heart."

"Herman Peterson?" Butch squinted. "Oh, the Hermit."

Herman Peterson had come to Santa Tierra after a tour of duty in the Great War a year or more ago. He had been injured and now walked with a fairly pronounced limp. His people were from Santa Fe or Albuquerque, as far as anyone knew, but he had come to Santa Tierra to live after he got out of the service.

He had stayed in the McLoughlin Boarding House for a time. After a while he either didn't have any money or else he couldn't stand being inside any more. So he ended up homeless. No doubt some thought he was lazy or a malingerer. Some thought he was crazy. Most knew he was suffering from shell shock or what they called soldier's heart. No one knew how to help him, and no one quite trusted him, including Butch.

After a few months of living in Santa Tierra, most people avoided him, and he avoided most people. He spent a lot of time wandering the desert or up in the woods. People forgot what he had been like before the war—if they had ever known—and Herman Peterson became known as The Hermit. Sometimes they called him "Hermit" as though it were his first name.

He did handyman work on some of the area ranches and used the money he earned to go to Angel's Heaven on Earth to drink too much. Sometimes Angel let him sleep it off on a cot in her storage room.

Once or twice Angel wouldn't fool around with Butch because Herman was sleeping on the cot in the hall between Angel's room and the saloon. Butch didn't understand what that had to do with anything, but she began to dislike this small blond man whose existence occasionally interfered with her love life.

Hunter had asked several times if the Hermit could come stay on the ranch. TomA said it was up to Butch, at least until after Wayward Art Spectacle.

"I don't want him working here," Butch said. "I don't trust him."

"Why? He was a soldier fighting for us," Hunter said, "and he got hurt. Shouldn't we take care of him?"

"Yes," Butch said. "The collective we should take care of

him. But I don't want him running around here, close to you and close to TomA's and Trick's valuables. Maybe he can come help out on the ranch after the Spectacle."

Hunter made a noise.

"You're not always right," Hunter said.

"Never said I was, darlin," Butch said. "George! You comin' or what?" Butch took Rosey's reins, bunched them up around the saddle horn, put her leg in the left stirrup, then pulled herself up and over the horse.

"We're all drifters," Hunter said. "We were all lost before we came here."

"I wasn't," Jimmy said.

Hunter glared at him.

"Well, I wasn't."

Butch felt sorry for Hunter. She was trying to make a point and her pretty (and dumb) boyfriend was making it difficult for her.

"I know," Butch said. "Let me think about it some. I'll get back to you."

"Might be too late by then," Hunter murmured.

George came toward them.

"What do you mean?" Butch asked.

"Nothing," Hunter said. "It's just that you used to be nicer. Now you're mean." She walked away from them. Jimmy shrugged and followed her. George got on Bucket.

Butch shook her head. She wondered what that was all about. Didn't matter right now. Now she had to go look at a dead man.

"Hope the sheriff has got him on ice," Butch said. "It's a hot one today."

Three

Butch debated with herself about whether she should stop into Angel's for a beer. Then she remembered she would have to see Angel. Now that she wasn't drunk, it stung more than a little bit that Angel had thrown her over for Merle T. Connelly. *Merle T. Connelly.* The thought of it made her a bit sick to her stomach.

Butch steered Rosey away from Angel's, which was where she was headed—out of habit, most likely—and went toward Doc Broome's office, which was where they had the body. Bucket was already trotting toward the doc's place. Guess he wasn't as used to going to Angel's as Rosey was.

George and Butch stopped in front of Doc Broome's, got off their horses, and looped the reins around the hitching post.

"Don't go anywhere, Rosey," Butch said. "I may need to gallop away from the scene of a crime."

George was already walking into the building. Butch patted Rosey's neck. Butch wasn't afraid of much, and she didn't get sick often, but she did not like the sight of blood and gore. Something about it made the bile rise in her. Pissed her off, since she was vaguely interested in what a bullet or cougar wound looked like. She took a deep breath, began to whistle, and took the steps two at a time.

Margaret Broome sat at a desk in the reception area and pointed to the back when Butch came in. Butch nodded and went down the hall, past the examination rooms, and into the coroner's room, which was slightly cooler than outside. The room was crowded with too many people, five of them alive—including Butch—and one of them dead, on the table, his shirt unbuttoned to expose a very white chest with a huge dark red hole in it.

Butch looked away from the wound.

"It stinks in here, Doc," she said. "A bath every once in a while wouldn't hurt you."

"You recognize this man, Butch?" Sheriff Carter asked.

The sheriff, Doc Broome, George, and some man Butch didn't know looked at her. The stranger looked vaguely familiar. Butch walked to the head of the man and looked down. It had been dark out. She hadn't been able to make out his features. But this man looked smaller, more slightly built than the one she'd nearly tripped over in the desert last night.

She wished someone had closed his eyes. They were either milky blue or clouding over with death. Was that what death was? Some kind of storm that took over the body and pushed the spirit out?

"I don't think I've ever seen this man before," Butch said.

"Let's go talk outside," Sheriff Carter said.

"Can we put him in the ground now?" Doc Broome asked as the others started to file out of the room. "It ain't me that needs a bath. He's stinking up the place."

Butch glanced back. "Naw, I think it's you, Doc."

"Gotta call the coroner's jury on this one," Carter said. "You know that, Doc."

The four of them stepped outside and stayed on the porch,

leaving Doc Broome in the room with the corpse.

"George, Butch, this here is Deputy Jonathan Fargo," Carter said. "He and Deputy Thomas Jones, in there, were following a bank robber up here from Nogales. Last night Deputy Fargo was attacked and knocked out. When he came to, he found his partner dead, not far from where he'd been attacked."

"Isn't this out of your jurisdiction?" Butch asked Deputy Fargo.

"We were gonna contact the sheriff in the morning, if we stopped here," Fargo said. "We've been traveling for days, trying to get the bank robber."

"And you think your bank robber is here?" George asked.

"We followed him here," Fargo said. "But we lost him for a couple of hours. And then it got dark and I got mugged."

That was why Butch thought she recognized him: He was the same build as the unconscious man in the desert—and he had the same smell. Like rotten meat, or something.

"You could have been mugged by anyone," Butch said. "Some drunk. Someone who thought you were after them."

"Like a bank robber?" Carter said. "This is murder, Butch. And kidnapping. If you saw anything last night, you need to tell us."

"I didn't see anything that would help you," Butch said. "I was half drunk. I thought I heard a scream in the distance, but that could have been Crazy Betty howling at the moon."

Butch could feel George's eyes on her. Why didn't she just tell them about Cruz?

"You said kidnapping?" George said.

Fargo nodded. He winced a bit and touched the top of his head.

"Yes, the bank robber kidnapped the daughter of a wealthy Mexican man," Fargo said. "He forced her to participate in the bank robbery."

"How do you force someone to participate in a bank robbery?" Butch asked.

"Who is this woman?" Fargo asked the sheriff. "Why is any of this her business? Is she the one who shot my partner?"

"Well, fuck you and the horse you rode in on," Butch said. "Who are you and why are you in our town? How do we know you didn't kill your own partner in some dispute over money or women? Or whatever."

Sheriff Carter put his hand up. "I checked his papers, Butch," Carter said. "He's legit, as far as I can tell. I've wired his boss. And Fargo, I told you before she arrived that some people saw Butch out in the desert last night. And Butch favors pistols, not rifles. Your deputy was killed by a rifle shot, I'll warrant."

George started fidgeting. Butch knew he was pissed off. He didn't like strangers much, and strangers who bad-mouthed her really pissed him off.

Sheriff Carter noticed George, too. "Hold on there, George. Deputy Fargo, I done told you that Butch and George here are responsible for the security of Wayward Ranch and they know this country better than anyone. They can track a beetle through dried mud and a jaguar through the air. If they were willing, they'd help you find your bank robber."

"I ain't saying I'm willing," Butch said. "I asked you a question. How'd this bank robber force a kidnapped woman to rob a bank?"

"He's a crack shot," Fargo said, "as you can see from the damage he did to my partner. He threatened to kill the woman if she didn't do as he asked. She told the teller that this Antonio Rodriguez had a bead drawn on her and if he didn't see them putting money into her carpet bag right away he was gonna kill her and then them all. And they could see the man, across the street, so they did what she asked and gave her what would fit into her bag. She left the bank and went into the stable across the street where the man was waiting, and they rode out of town. No one has seen them since. He has either hidden her somewhere or he has killed her. We think we tracked him here."

"Maybe they were working together," George said.

"We considered that," Fargo said, "but she was a devoted daughter and mother. Why would she help this man? The bank teller said she was quite distraught. She whispered, 'Tell my son I love him.' That doesn't sound like an accomplice to me. What if he dragged her off and left her in the desert somewhere to die? We need to find her."

"And the money," Butch said.

"Of course we want the money back," Fargo said. Butch thought he sounded more irritated than he should. "But the woman is what we're most concerned about."

"I can tell you this," Butch said, "I do not recognize your poor dead partner. And I am sorry for his demise. As we wander to and fro today, I will endeavor to look for this young woman and the bank robber, since everyone has asked so nice."

"That's all we can ask," Sheriff Carter said. "Keep in touch."

George didn't wait for any good-bye pleasantries. He stepped off the porch and got up on Bucket. Carter took Butch's right arm and pulled her out of Fargo's earshot.

"I gotta tell you," he said, "I've heard reports that Jezebel is back. We got the ditch cleaning coming up. I don't want Jezebel deciding to come into town to lunch on someone while that's happening. Anything you can do about it?"

"Carter, if someone saw a jaguar it ain't Jezebel," Butch said. "If it was, she'd be so old she'd be toothless by now. And jaguars don't eat people besides."

Carter raised his eyebrows in a kind of shrug. "Stranger things have happened in these parts. And we all know she follows you from here to there."

Butch shook her head. She didn't know how to argue with that kind of logic. Jezebel had never been in town to be out of town. She wasn't a human being.

She wasn't even Jezebel.

Plus wild animals didn't go around hunting people. It was the other way around.

"I'll keep an eye out," Butch said. "By the way, did you find anything in the desert around the body? Shell casings? Pieces of clothing?"

"No, we didn't find anything," Carter said. "Barely found any tracks. You're welcome to go search yourself. I put a stake and a flag in the ground where we found Deputy Jones. Quite a bit of blood. We talked to the folks who live around there, Crazy Betty, the Jacksons, Mildred and Ben. They all heard some animals, and maybe some arguing, but they couldn't be sure. That reminds me, Crazy Betty wants to talk to you."

"Me? Why?"

Butch did not particularly relish spending time with Crazy Betty. She always had something to complain about, especially strange lights in the sky. Crazy Betty was certain people from Mars or Venus or somewhere were dropping down into the area for a visit. If she wasn't blathering on about that, she wanted to talk about old loves. She claimed Ambrose Bierce as one of her last conquests.

"He never went to Mexico that last year, you know," Crazy Betty told Butch a few years earlier. "He was right here. We did the wild for days. Then the space touristas took him." That's what she called the visitors from the stars: space touristas who came to Earth for a vacation.

"Does she know something about Deputy Jones being shot?" Butch asked.

"She didn't say."

Butch looked at him.

"I asked!" he said. "She said it was important that she talk to you, so I'm giving you the message."

"Do you know anything about this Herman Peterson character?" Butch asked. "They call him The Hermit."

"I know him," Carter said. "I know his family. They're good people. He had a bad time in the war, like so many. Some people come home with their lungs fucked up, others with their brains scrambled. Herman's not all back from the war yet, that's all."

"No trouble with the law since he come here?"

Carter shook his head. "Nothing like that. Why?"

"Just asking," Butch said. "Hunter is out trying to do good deeds, I guess. Wants me to hire him. I've said no. She thinks I'm being mean. You know kids."

"Yep," Carter said. "I can't say in public what my kids have thought about me over the years. They say I've ignored them and I don't respect them. Fortunately, I don't pay any attention to what they say, so it don't bother me none."

Butch laughed. "I hear ya."

Butch stepped off the porch and walked over to Rosey. As she grabbed the reins, she looked at the sheriff and Fargo.

"What kind of horse did your partner have?" Butch asked.

"A brown mare," Fargo said. "Haven't seen hide nor hair of her."

"Good to know," Butch said.

She got on Rosey, touched her hat, and turned Rosey to follow George who was already way ahead of her. When she caught up to him, she said. "What is wrong with you?"

"Fargo's an asshole," George said. "And so are you. Why are you protecting Cruz? He's probably the bank robber, killer, and the kidnapper."

"I'm not protecting him," Butch said. "I'm giving him the benefit of the doubt. Over the years, we've been accused of things we didn't do."

"And never accused of things we did do," George said.

The horses trotted through town. Butch raised her hand now and again to wave to this or that person. TomA was always encouraging her to be friendly, even when she wasn't drunk. He said it was good for her to be social, and her sociability would reflect well on Wayward Ranch.

Butch knew TomA didn't really care about that last part. He wanted Butch to be happy, and TomA equated happiness with love. He naturally thought a more pleasant Butch might attract to her a permanent love interest.

"We may have had our problems when we were children," George said, "but we never robbed a bank or kept anyone prisoner."

"A prisoner of love, maybe," Butch said. George didn't say anything. Butch laughed. "Why are you so grumpy, George? It's like I'm living with an old man."

George shook his head. "I feel like I haven't been out in the wild much. This city living makes me itchy."

"This ain't city living," Butch said. "Not even close to any kind of city. But I hear ya. After the Wayward Art Spectacle and after the ditches are cleaned, we can go."

"I was thinking I might go now," he said. "And go alone."

Butch turned Rosey so they were headed in the direction of the boarding house.

Butch cleared her throat. "Sure, George. You do whatever you like. I know you like to be out there yippin' with the coyotes."

George didn't say anything. Butch listened to the clip clop of the horses' hooves on the hard dirt road.

"Noticed things are changing, Butch?" George said.

"You were complaining that I was doing too much of the same thing," Butch said.

George looked at her. Butch grinned.

"Where are we going?" George asked.

"To the boarding house," Butch said. "I want to see if that Hermit character is hanging around. Or is that not what you meant?"

They stopped the horses in front of the McLoughlin Boarding house, dismounted, tied the horses up, and then went through the open door into the dark house. When Butch's eyes adjusted to the dark, she saw Mrs. McLoughlin pushing a mop over the stone floor.

"Keeping the dust down," Mrs. McLoughlin said without looking up at them. "It's April and I'm keeping the dust down. You need something?"

"Wondering if Herman Peterson is still staying here," Butch said. "Heard he was looking for work."

Mrs. McLoughlin stopped mopping and looked up at them. "He was here and then he wasn't. Even when he was here he wasn't here."

"But has he been here and not here lately?" Butch asked.

"Been gone for a while now," Mrs. McLoughlin said. "I don't think he's coming back. You know his daddy has a horse business a little south of Santa Fe. Herman was one of those so-called natural horsemen. Learned it through his blood, all the way back to Ireland. Probably some leprechaun told him how to weave a spell so the horses would do whatever he wanted them to do." She chuckled. "Not that he told me none of this. Heard it around. And his daddy came looking for him one time after he got back from the war. Found him. Herman didn't want to go back."

"George has been teaching horses natural since he was a boy," Butch said.

She nodded. "I know it. Just saying if you needed help with all those horses you got, you might want to ask Herman, if you can find him. Tell him I said hey."

She looked away from them and started to push the mop around again.

Butch and George glanced at one another and then turned to leave.

"Why you looking for him anyway?" Mrs. McLoughlin asked.

Butch and George stopped and turned around again.

"He in trouble?" she asked. "I heard they found a dead man just outside of town, dying out in the moonlight with the coyotes howling all around him and Crazy Betty screamin' for them all to shut up."

"Naw, he ain't in trouble. Hunter thought he might need help and I wasn't much open to it, so now she's mad at me."

Mrs. McLoughlin nodded. "Yep, you always had a soft spot for that girl. She's a little younger than—" She stopped. "You tell them all I said hey. Sonny Boy will be down at the ditch in place of his daddy. I'll have fixings for all. Some things change but some things never change. Gotta clean the ditch. Gotta wash this floor."

Butch had forgotten Mr. McLoughlin had passed away last year. She looked at George. Maybe that was why Mrs. McLoughlin seemed so strange today.

"You need anything?" George asked.

She looked up at them again. A stray hair fell down over her forehead. She pushed it out of the way.

"Naw," she said. "People have been real good to me. Your momma and some of your people even came, you know, George. Appreciated it. It's the silence sometimes. Mr. McLoughlin made noises all the time. Used to irritate me some. I would sing so I wouldn't hear all his little noises some mornings." She shrugged. "Now I don't have any reason to sing." She smiled. "He told me once that sometimes he made noises he knew I didn't like just so he could hear me sing. Appreciated all the times TomA came to see me since, always sent your regards, too, Butch. It is the kindnesses that get us through the ugly. Go on now." She waved at them. "I gots to finish this floor before a new layer of dust falls."

Butch and George backed out, waved, went outside.

"Shit," Butch said as she got on Rosey. "I had forgotten about the mister. Hope the missus is all right."

George got on Bucket and they headed out of town. They didn't say anything until they were riding through a cotton-wood grove near the acequia. A crow called out, somewhere in the branches of one of the trees. Sounded like the crow said, *"Home."*

Butch waved.

"You think you'll ever love anyone that much?" Butch asked. "She's like a completely different person now. I don't want to love anyone like that. Take your heart with them when they die. I mean I'd like to smother myself in Angel's bosom again one day, but—" Butch shook her head and patted Rosey's neck. She had been sad when her mother died. Hadn't she? Too young to know. And when Grandma Crow died? She had been sad to see Grandma Crow go, but she did not miss Grandma No One.

A coyote crossed the road in front of them, about fifty feet away. The coyote stopped when she got to the other side and looked at them for a second. Butch stared right back at her. The coyote looked like she had something to say.

Apparently she thought better of it, because she trotted off into the scrub.

A road runner followed a few seconds later. The bird stopped and looked at Butch. *"Know the way."*

"I ain't lost," Butch called. "I know the way. Otherwise I'd follow you."

Grandma Crow had told her road runners could lead you to safety if you were lost, even though their X-marks-the-spot prints were somewhat confusing. If you weren't lost, best not to follow them. Although they would protect you from evil spirits.

"You didn't answer me, George," Butch said.

"I'm trying to ignore you," he said. "It's such a beautiful day, I was hoping not to hear any more of your yatter."

Butch laughed.

"For another thing," George said, "you know everything about my life. You could answer that question better than anyone."

"What question?" she said. "I've forgotten what the heck we were discussing." She laughed. "I know that you'd be lost without me, Mr. George. I know you'd be pushing around the mop all lost and lonesome without yours truly."

"Yep, I'd be mopping all right," he said. "Mopping up whatever mess you left behind."

"Ouch," Butch said. "That almost sounds bitter, George. I've never known you to be bitter. Laconic, but not bitter. If I'm getting on your nerves, maybe you should go out somewhere and get your mind right."

"It ain't you," he said. "There's this woman on the pueblo."

"You fancy her?" Butch asked.

"She's a good woman," he said. "And it's what the family wants. I had those bad years when I was drinking and causing trouble. Now that's all mended, so they want me to come home."

"They think I've taken you down the wrong road," Butch said.

"You haven't taken me anywhere," he said. "For one thing, I've never followed anyone, which was part of the problem." He looked at her. "But you know all this. Don't know what's gotten into me."

"I been feeling the same way," Butch said. "Thinking about

the past. Grandma No One. The school. Going back to Pueblo land when they kicked me out. You taking me in. Don't see much sense in ruminating about none of it, but there it is."

Butch looked around. In the distance, the mountains looked like dark blue shadows under the clouds, like ghost mountains, neither here nor there. Above, the sky was a perfect blue, holding all the good luck in the world. Butch knew why she stayed living in this place every time she gazed up at that sky: like a round blue door to happiness. The air smelled like spring today even though Butch couldn't place any particular scent—maybe it was just the scent of water still in the air after the recent rains. A rabbit ran beside the horses for a bit and then dashed under a marigold bush growing along the almost-road they were traveling.

"I need to give them an answer," he said. "It's only fair to her."

"You wanna say yes, you say yes," Butch said. "I'd love to be an aunt to your children. I look forward to the day I can teach them my wild ways."

George laughed. Butch smiled. George didn't laugh often, even though he was a funny man—at least around Butch he was funny. Around other people, he didn't say much, not until he knew someone long and hard. Butch and George had been through so much together she wouldn't even know where to begin to reminisce about her life with him.

"If you have high regard for her and that's what you want to do," Butch said, "go on ahead."

"Don't push me," George said, "just cuz you want to live alone."

Butch shook her head. "I don't want to live alone," she said. "Who'd kick my ass out of bed? Who'd make me breakfast? Who'd hold my hair when I threw up?"

"I got more hair than you do," George said, "and you really

should learn to cook. It's a shame when a person can't take care of herself."

"I can take care of myself," Butch said.

"Yeah, I know," George said. "But you can't cook."

They were silent again. Butch heard only the sound of the horse hooves and the wind through the cottonwoods they were passing. Something about cottonwoods was always pleasing to Butch. Maybe it was because wherever cottonwoods grew, she knew water could not be far away. Maybe it was because her momma's last breath intermingled with an old cottonwood. Maybe it was because Butch's first kiss happened beneath a cottonwood.

"It would be a lot easier if we got married," George said. "I mean, if we felt that way about each other. Then this kind of thing wouldn't come up."

Butch shrugged. "I suppose," she said. "But we don't feel that way. I mean, we're both partial to women. Not a match made in heaven. And why the hell are we talking about this? I don't want to have any serious conversations when I'm this sober. Can't you wait until I'm drunk again?"

"Don't you ever think about your future?" George asked. "Don't you ever wonder about how we live?"

"No," Butch said, "and no. What the hell is the matter with the way we live? We've got a good life, a happy life. You've never had any doubts before."

"I've had doubts every day of my life since I met you," George said. "When I came out the door of Grandma Crow's house and saw you standing there out in the desert like you were, all bloody, all lost and ragged, I knew my life had changed."

Butch felt her face flush. She wished she had a drink.

"Goddamn it, George," Butch said. "I don't want to talk about this. Got nothing to do with my life now. Nothing. Leave it alone."

"I should have been able to do more," George said.

"What the fuck are you talking about?" Butch said. "No, never mind. I don't want to know. You did everything you could for me when I needed it, better than anyone else. Now we've got our lives. These trips into the past, I don't know what they're about, but I don't like 'em."

"Fuck," George said.

"You got some notion about what I want or who you think I would have become if things had been different?" Butch asked. "That's complete bullshit. This is who I am. Wouldn't be any different if they hadn't kicked me out of St. Anne's. Wouldn't have been any different if I hadn't let Suzanne's brother fuck me that night in the dormitory. No different. The sun would still be shining on a day like today, and I'd still be riding down this road with you. You might believe we would have never met but you'd be wrong. I don't believe in destiny or any of that shit, but we were destined to be compadres, come hell or high water. Only thing different would be that we would not be having this argument. That is for sure."

"This isn't an argument," George said. "This is what normal people call a conversation."

"Normal people?" Butch made a noise. "What the fuck do we have in common with normal people? This yammering is exhausting me. I feel like I've done nothing but talk all day. I need some action. Let's go eat some of Maria's fine cooking and then decide where we're gonna go look for Jezebel and Deputy Tommy Jones's killer."

"Tommy Jones?" George said. "Thought that Fargo asshole said his name was Thomas Jones. Didn't look like a Tommy to me. Have to be more amiable looking—"

"Oh fer chrissakes," Butch said. "Yeee haw! Come on, Rosey. Can't shut him up so let's try to outrun him."

Four

George took the horses to the stable, once he and Butch had dismounted. Butch wanted to talk to Mateo Cruz alone, which was convenient since Bandito was sitting under the big old piñon tree not far from the Big House, just watching Butch walk toward him. Butch could hardly believe how beautiful this man was as he leaned back in his chair next to a wooden table with a huge yellow sunflower painted on the top of it. Butch looked into Mateo's big black eyes. She could not remember the last time she had found a man attractive. Besides George, of course, but she would never admit that to anyone. And that guy from California she'd had an all-nighter with a few years ago.

Mateo smiled at her. Something not quite right about his smile. It was sad. He was hiding something still.

Wasn't everyone?

Butch cleared her throat. She had never fallen for a pretty face before, and she wasn't going to now.

Well, maybe she fell but only long enough to be a little bit naked with the owner of the pretty face.

Man, she wished she could see Angel tonight.

Butch took off her hat and slapped it against her leg.

"So here's what's going on," Butch said to Mateo. "We found your horse, the Appaloosa. You saw him?"

Mateo nodded.

Butch said, "They've got a dead deputy they found out with the yucca and bear grass. Shot last night. I talked to a Deputy Fargo and saw a dead Deputy Tommy Jones. He was out near where I found you. Did you shoot him?"

"What?" Mateo asked.

Butch sat on one of the chairs near the sunflower table. She ran her hand across the table and looked up in the piñon tree and saw a magpie looking down at her. She wondered if the bird was building a nest or spying on the humans.

Butch looked at Mateo, but he avoided her eyes. "I want to know if you killed that man."

Mateo sat forward. "Of course not," he said. "You were with me. I didn't have a gun."

"You could have tossed it," Butch said.

"Did you find a gun anywhere near him?" Mateo asked.

"No," Butch said.

"And you didn't find a gun on me," Mateo said. "I didn't shoot anyone."

"The deputies were following a bank robber," Butch said. "Seems a strange coincidence that they were chasing a bank robber and you at the same time."

"Maybe they got us mixed up," he said. "I didn't shoot anyone. I didn't kill anyone."

"The bank robber kidnapped the daughter of a rich Mexican," Butch said. "They want her back. They think she might be dead or locked up somewhere. You know anything about that?"

Butch watched Mateo's face to see if anything changed. Did his eyes shift away from her? His mouth twitched. And his right hand—the one that wasn't in the sling—gripped the chair.

"I did not kidnap some rich Mexican woman," he said. "I have one goal only. I want my son. Period. I was trying to escape the men who were after me. Maybe they were these same men, these so-called deputies. Maybe they are lying to you, trying to trick you into turning me over to them."

"Would you talk with the deputy, this Fargo guy?" Butch asked.

Mateo sighed and looked away. Then he looked back at Butch.

"No," he said. "Then everyone will know where I am, including those who are hunting me. I only want my son. I will get better and then continue my quest. If you don't have any more questions for me, I'm going inside. Maria said dinner would be ready soon."

Mateo pushed himself up with his free hand and then walked away from Butch. George passed him and came over to the table and sat on it and put his feet on a nearby chair.

"You believe him?" George asked.

"I guess I believe he didn't kill anyone. The rest I don't know."

"Why do you believe him?" George asked. "Because he's pretty?"

"Naw," Butch said. "I figure since the new husband is rich and Mateo ain't, Mateo was coming out at the little end of the horn. And I don't like seeing a parent separated from his child, that's all."

George looked at her. She squinted up at the sun.

"Been a long day," Butch said, "and I haven't even been awake that long. Feel like I need a drink. Like a whole saloon of drinkin'. I guess I gotta find a new place now that Angel and I are no longer. Maybe one of them places on the plaza. Lot of strangers and artist types, but maybe we can kill some of 'em and make room for us."

George smiled.

"What are you grinning about?" Butch asked.

"I was imagining all the Spanish and the English and who-ever else gone from here," George said. "Just felt kind of peaceful."

Butch rolled her eyes. "Well, you're about three hundred, four hundred years too late. I think we're here to stay."

"We'll see," George said. "We are a very patient people."

"Hey, you scoundrels!"

Butch looked toward the house. Agica Vasquez was walking toward them. Today she wore a bright blue dress that almost matched the color of the sky. Her brown hair was pulled back from her face. Butch always thought Agica looked strange in a dress. She didn't think that about other women, but Agica was different. It was as though she was in a costume every time she wore a dress. Maybe it was because Butch had spent many hours out in the bush with her. When they were younger, Agica had taught Butch to be a better shot, and Butch had taught Agica how to be a better tracker.

George got off the table and gave Agica a hug and a peck on the cheek. Agica blushed. Butch wanted to smack George. He accused *her* of being unfeeling. Agica had a long-standing crush on George, which he did not reciprocate. He liked her, but she was just Agica to him, his old friend.

Everyone thought of Agica as the librarian because she bought and sold books, lent books, too, and she was the curator for the Wayward Art Spectacle every year. Agica knew a lot about almost everything.

Butch thought of her as a big sister, even though she was probably a couple of years younger than Butch. She had been engaged years earlier, was all dressed up and ready to go to church and tie the knot, but her betrothed went and ran off with some floozy from Roswell. Agica had kept to herself for a while after that. And pretty much never opened her heart up to anyone again. She wasn't bitter, she said; she was careful.

"Hey, Aggie," Butch said. "You getting ready for the Spectacle so soon?"

Usually Agica participated in all the ceremonies and rituals that went along with the annual ditch cleaning. After the ditch cleaning—*la limpia de la acequia*—Agica started organizing the art that artists from all over the area had either dropped off at the ranch themselves or sent in by messenger.

"Yep, I'm trying to get a jump on it," Agica said. "And I wanted to let you know there have been some thefts around town."

George and Butch looked at one another.

"Something for the sheriff to look into?" George asked.

"I told Deputy Paper," Agica said. "He said it was nothing."

"He's a half-wit," Butch said. "And that's being generous. What kind of thefts?"

"Strange stuff," Agica said. "An old doll someone was about to throw out. Toy horses. A small stuffed bird. A dog collar, from Gomez's dead dog Dottie. My father's old inkwell disappeared."

"Dead dog Dottie?" Butch said. "Say that five times real fast."

"Dottie dog dead," George said.

Agica gave them a look.

"Aggie, why are you telling us these things?" Butch asked. "What's it got to do with us or Wayward Ranch?"

"Just thought you'd like to know something untoward may be happening," Agica said. "I wouldn't want a piece of artwork to go missing. That's your bailiwick."

Butch nodded. "Okay, sister. Sounds like whoever the thief is, they're collecting junk, not art."

"I beg your pardon," Agica said. "That inkwell meant a great deal to me."

"I'm sorry," Butch said. "I didn't realize. I've seen it sitting on your desk. It's as dry as . . . as I am right now. Had a crack in it and it was dusty most of the time."

"All that is true," Agica said. "But I still care about it."

"You want me to try and track down your inkwell?" Butch asked. "Is that what this is all about?"

"She's givin' us a heads up," George said. "That's all. There's some kind of thief running around town. We should know it. Thank you, Aggie."

"Oh lord," Butch said. "Why are you two being so polite with each other? Did you hit the sheets together and forget to tell me?"

George held out his arm to Agica. "Shall we go into dinner, Agica, and leave the riffraff out here?"

Agica took George's arm, and they began walking toward the house.

"I hate it when you talk like white people," Butch shouted. "I bet that's why Jezebel is after us! She can't stand you being a turncoat!"

Butch laughed as the two kept walking.

She laughed, but she didn't think it was funny.

Something about people pretending to be something they weren't got her goat.

It made her think of the nuns at St. Anne's Home for Wayward Boys. And the parents of the boys who were sent there. Some of the boys came from rich families—none of them or their families had thought much of Butch.

She looked around. On a day like today, Wayward Ranch seemed perfect. An eagle was flying above a grove of aspens out past the meadow, the meadow that was purple and yellow now with wildflowers, probably desert marigolds and lupines.

Some of the horses George had been working with were grazing in the small pastures closer to the barn. Rosey and Bucket were amongst them. They had a sedating effect on the more wild horses. And the piñon tree near Butch smelled a bit like pitch today. Or maybe just spring. The magpie was still looking at her.

"You got something to say to me?" Butch asked.

The magpie cocked her head.

"Go home."

Butch nodded. "I've heard that before," she said. "But this is home. What else you got for me?"

"Rrrrrring."

"An alarm clock?" Butch said. "If you're going to come into my daydreams or my reality or whatever this is, you need to be clearer. I don't understand subtle."

The magpie flew away.

"How rude," Butch said. She rubbed her face.

She had thought of Wayward Ranch as her home for years. Lately, she kept remembering what it had been like when it was St. Anne's Home for Wayward Boys.

She did not like those memories.

She did not like cogitating on them. Didn't like chewing on them like some gristle she should spit out and be done with.

Before it was Wayward Ranch it had been St. Anne's Home for Wayward Boys. Before that, the land and buildings were abandoned for a time. It may even have been owned by a Mexican businessman. Legend was that in the distant past an Englishman who loved art and artists had owned it and called it Wayward Ranch. TomA and Trick had decided legend was history, and they wanted to relive that particular history of the ranch, whether it be truth or fable.

When Butch first came to St. Anne's after Grandma Crow died, the place had been a complex of buildings sprawled over a meadow that had been trampled down by horses and cattle over the years. Beyond the buildings, a woodland forest edged away from St. Anne's as more and more trees were cut down.

The priest had lived in the main house. The nuns lived in a smaller house not far away. The boys had their own dormitory that was hot in the summer and cold in the winter. And no matter how much the nuns made the boys clean the dorm, it always smelled like boy, at least to Butch. She wasn't allowed in the dormitory except when Sister Claw or Father Brufield was punishing her. Once Butch hit puberty and started looking more like a girl, Sister Claw sometimes locked her in the dormitory with the boys as a punishment for her and as a temptation for the boys.

The first time Sister Claw locked her in the dormitory, Butch was afraid. She stood near the door and looked into the sea of boy faces in the semi-darkness. She knew enough about the boys at St. Anne's to know she should be afraid. Some of them were local boys who were always in trouble. Some were boys from back East who weren't living up to the expectations of their parents, and most of them were very angry that they'd been sent away to this dry, desolate place. These two groups— the Easters and the Westers—were always fighting with one another and plotting revenge on one another. They coalesced into a single group when they tried to make Butch's life miserable.

Over the years, Butch had beat the shit out of one boy after another. Each time she got into a fight with a boy, Father Brufield or Sister Claw whipped her. Father Brufield said she shouldn't fight. It wasn't ladylike.

Butch said to him, "You bet your ass I'm not ladylike, Father sir. You want me alive or you want me a lady?"

Locked in the dormitory that first time, Butch was wary. Sister Claw had admonished the boys that if any of them touched Butch, they would be punished. Butch could tell from the silence that most of them were trying to decide if it would be worth the beating.

"Listen to me, boys," Butch hissed into the darkness that first time. "I won't tell Sister Claw if you come my way. I promise. I don't really care if you want to have a look-see. Or even a touch. But I feel it is my Christian duty to tell you what really happened to Bobby Keenan."

Bobby Keenan had left the school screaming in agony early one morning. The nuns told everyone that he had gotten bitten by a scorpion. On his penis. What they didn't tell everyone—because they didn't know—was that Butch had found a couple of scorpions and had put them into Bobby's pants. She had told him to leave her alone repeatedly, but he was older than the other boys and felt like she was his. And she had no say in the matter as far as he was concerned. Well, that was not an attitude Butch was going to tolerate.

Bobby never returned to the school after his unfortunate encounter with the scorpions.

"He got bit by a scorpion," a voice came out of the darkness.

"That's what they told you," Butch said. "The real truth is that Bobby and I had sex. Or tried to. He didn't know what he was doing, so he wasn't able to get past the teeth. Nothing I could do about the teeth myself since it is up to the man to soften them up. Bobby did not know what he was doing."

"Teeth? What teeth?" A squeaky voice.

"You know," Butch said. She whispered, "The teeth in my woman's part. Them teeth is pretty mighty. Especially in teenagers. I have to be careful even when I wipe myself."

Hushed silence.

"She's making that up," someone said.

Butch shrugged in the darkness. "Suit yourself. I thought I should tell you. I don't think I'll ever forgive myself for what happened to Bobby. Last I heard, half his penis dropped off. They don't think he'll ever have children. Hell, he won't ever have sex again. It's a shame. He had potential, that one."

Butch was thirteen years old by then, but she had lived with Grandma No One for most of those years.

None of the boys bothered Butch that night, but she stayed awake the whole time to make certain. The next time Sister Claw locked her in the dormitory, Butch had a knife. She made sure the boys knew she had it. And they already knew she could use it. Father Brufield had whipped her bloody for using it on Joe Kelly. She didn't understand what all the fuss was about: She had barely nicked him.

"I was warning him to leave me alone," Butch said. "These boys of yours ain't no picnic, you know."

Father Brufield had stared at her for a moment. Then he shook his head and whipped her some more.

After each beating, Butch went into the kitchen and Maria made her something to eat and told her a story. When she first got to St. Anne's, Butch ran away a lot. But no one in town wanted to take care of her, so they brought her back to St. Anne's.

After a while, Butch stopped running. She liked Maria's food and stories too much. And as Butch got a little older, she figured out how to be invisible so that the nuns practically forgot about her. Most of the time.

They didn't lock her up with the boys very often. The last time they did it, during the summer when it was still light out, Butch decided to take off her shirt so she could keep cool in the stifling dormitory. The hootin', hollerin', and screaming tipped off Sister Claw that something was up. She dragged a laughing Butch out of the dormitory.

They went back to locking her up in the main house. Father Brufield was away more than he was at the house. When he was gone, if Sister Claw was annoyed with Butch, she would lock her up in the attic room all by herself.

The first night Butch was afraid because she had heard the house was haunted. And she did hear some strange noises. Sounded like a squirrel was in the walls or someone was whispering in her ear. She said to the noise, "You might as well come out and conversate with me, cuz I grew up with Grandma No One and nothing you can do will scare me."

Unless the noise was the ghost of Grandma No One. That thought left her shivering for a while, but then she started talking to it. "What are you still doing here anyway, whoever you are? You can't want to be here with those stinky boys or those cruel women. Can't be here for Maria's cooking cuz you can't eat. The afterlife has got to be more interesting than this. No? Well, let me tell you about my life."

Butch was ten the first time they locked her in the attic. After that she pretended she was afraid, but she wasn't. Maria had passed her a skeleton key so she was able to get out of the locked room and come and go as she wished. Each time, as soon as Sister Claw was out of the house, Butch unlocked the attic door and then she wandered the empty house by herself, talking to the noise or the ghost or whatever it was. If Maria was still there, in the kitchen, Butch would sit by the door and listen to her cleaning up or murmuring to herself.

Sometimes Butch would sit in the Big Room and imagine what it would be like if she owned this house. First she would throw out all the dark furniture. And she'd opened the windows so she could see outside. The mountains were just visible in the distance. Why wouldn't they want to see that every morning when they woke up? She would bring in plants and animals. They would be welcome in her home any time. And her tatters box would be up on the mantle, in a place of honor, where she could see it any time, like the mountains.

And no boys would ever be allowed in her house. In her beloved house.

A couple years after the nuns kicked Butch out and she went back to live in Grandma Crow's old home (with George), she returned to St. Anne's with the intention of burning the place to the ground.

She stood on the threshold of the land, woozy from drink, furious at what the nuns had done to her, and she wanted revenge. Yet she stared into the semi-darkness at the main house and she remembered it with fondness, as if she were remembering an old friend. Then TomA came out of the house and offered her a place to stay. She accepted his offer. No one could refuse TomA anything. He could charm the scales off a mermaid. Or a fish. Or any other kind of being with scales.

Butch soon learned that one of the boys had burned down the dormitory not long after the nuns kicked Butch out. She couldn't imagine who would have had enough nerve to do that. And soon after that, St. Anne's had closed. TomA, an artist from New York city or Boston, or some place back East, bought the place, and he and Patrick began renovating.

The first thing they did was open all the windows. Then they gave away the dark furniture. They tore down walls and made small rooms big. Trick began painting *trompe l'oeils* on some of the walls, mostly city streets turning to mountains, deserts, or meadows.

Then they cleared out the old adobe buildings that had been around for centuries, and one of those eventually became Butch's home. Butch's and George's, when he showed up looking for her.

Butch still loved the Big House, but she wanted to live in the adobe casita. It felt more like her style.

Butch blinked and suddenly realized Archie had pushed his nose against her leg. She patted his head and breathed deeply.

"This is horseshit," Butch said. "Why after all these years am I thinking about any of this?"

Archie whimpered.

"Yeah, you want to be out in the wild, too," Butch said. "Just like George. And me. I guess." She looked around. "Where I really want to be is home." Her throat tightened. "Thought this was home. Went to sleep two nights ago and this was home." What had happened between then and now? Angel had sent her packing; Mateo Cruz had arrived; Tommy Jones was gunned down and killed; George had threatened to run off and get married.

But Angel had tried to brush her off before. Strangers arrived at Wayward Ranch all the time. Strangers died in the desert a little less frequently than they arrived at the ranch. On occasion, George had muttered something about getting married and having children.

So it couldn't be any of that.

Who cared what had caused it? A night with Angel and a bottle of mezcal would stop it.

The magpie flew back into the piñon tree. Archie and Butch looked up at her.

"Be clear or be gone," Butch said.

The magpie continued to stare, cocking her head now and again.

Butch looked toward the house. She could hear laughter. She loved Maria's dinners. She loved being with everyone gathered around the big table.

Tonight she couldn't make herself stand up and go toward the house. She was tempted to saddle up Rosey and ride out into the desert and find Jezebel, if Jezebel was out there. She wouldn't mind missing the ditch cleaning and its rituals and ceremonies this year. She usually enjoyed the festivities. She always enjoyed watching other people work. In years past, she had even helped out when TomA didn't have enough strong bodies.

This year she liked the idea of being alone out in the desert or in the mountains.

She had wrestled with melancholy a few times over her life. Not that anyone knew about it. She usually just drank it down to the ground. Either that or it went away on its own.

She hoped another bout was not coming her way.

Maybe that was why she didn't want Hermit around—Herman Peterson. He made her think of her mother hanging from the cottonwood tree. She saw him and wondered if one day she'd be riding through the woods or along the riverside and she'd hear the crows cawing out a mourning song for him as he swung from some old river tree. She'd have to cut him down. Just as someone had had to cut down her mother.

Butch sat up straight. Why had she never thought of that before? Had Grandma Crow cut down her mother? Had she called on other people to do it?

Who would know the answers to these questions? Doc Broome? Who else? That was thirty-five years ago, give or take.

She rubbed the top of Archie's head.

What did it matter who had cut her mother down?

"Hey, Butch, we can't keep waitin' on you," Hunter shouted as she hurried toward her. "We're hungry."

Archie ran toward Hunter who was scowling at Butch. Seemed lately she was mad at Butch a great deal of the time.

Or maybe it was the teenage years. Butch had been angry when she was a teen. What did Hunter have to be angry about? She had everything.

"Darlin', why are you always snappin' at me?" Butch asked. She got up and met the teen. "I'm comin'. I didn't know you were waiting on me."

"I'm not always snapping at you," Hunter said. "That's an exaggeration. I get irritated with you for very specific things."

"If your irritation has anything to do with Herman Peterson, I was looking for him this afternoon. Thought I might give him a chance. TomA could use another worker or two for the ditch digging." Butch shrugged. "If I coulda found him, I would have told him."

"That's kind of you," Hunter said. "I'll try to find Herman and tell him. He sure could use the money. I like it when you're kind, Butch. I don't like it when you hate everyone in the world."

Butch flinched.

"I can't think of a single person I hate," Butch said. "Why would you say that?"

Hunter put her arm through Butch's. "You sure are sensitive lately," Hunter said. "What's wrong with you?"

Butch glanced at Hunter. She was getting so grown-up.

"You feel at home here, girl?" Butch asked. "Are you happy?" They stopped by the steps that led into the house.

"Sure I'm happy. And I feel at home because it is my home. Why? Don't you feel at home here? You've been here longer than any of us."

"No reason," Butch said. "Let's go eat. I don't know why you're delaying our entrance into the house. They're all waitin' on us, and I'm going to blame you."

Five

Butch fell right to sleep. This surprised her; it had been a while since she had gone to sleep without the benefit of alcohol or lovin' from Angel or some other lucky person. She had no dreams. She heard a coyote yipping and then whispering in her ear, *"Go."*

When she opened her eyes, it was just after dawn and Archie was sitting near her bed.

"Don't be talkin' to me so early in the morning," Butch said.

She leaned over and kissed the dog's muzzle. Then she got out of bed. She put on a clean undershirt, button-down shirt, and jeans.

If she was going out hunting for Jezebel today, she had better look good for her.

She walked by George's room and saw his bed was empty. She was rarely able to get up earlier than George. He had always been up before the sun.

Maybe he was the one responsible for the sun coming up each morning.

She went outside to greet the day. It was chilly, but the morning was already golden. The cottonwoods across the pasture were draped in sweet light.

Butch stretched and yawned, wondered if Maria was up yet, if breakfast was ready. Maybe she should go back into the casita and make breakfast herself to prove to George she could do it.

Naw. That wouldn't be good for anyone.

Least of all her.

She heard someone clear his throat. She turned around to face the Big House. Mateo Cruz was sitting at the table again. Even at the butt crack of dawn, Cruz was a good looking man. Must be his age. Young people always looked good no matter what.

It was disgusting.

"What are you doing up so early?" Butch asked. "You're lucky I didn't come out of the casita buck naked and scare the man right out of you."

Mateo laughed. Butch smiled.

"Couldn't be that bad," Mateo said.

"I've got my scars," Butch said. "How's your arm?"

"Good," he said. "I think. Trick will look at it today. But I think I'll stay a few days. Until that deputy moves on. Wouldn't want him thinking I was his bank robber. Wish I could do something to help around here. With this bullet hole in my arm, I'm a bit useless."

Butch sat next to Mateo on the bench.

"Naw," Butch said. "You can sit around and look pretty. Nothing to be done for a few days except ditch cleaning, and you look a little soft for that anyway, even if you hadn't been shot."

Mateo laughed again. "You sure know how to build up a man," he said.

"Most men don't need building up," Butch said. "Most of them need tearing down. Well, maybe not most, but quite a few of them. They think they own the world. Think they're on top of the world. Better they know that ain't true before we're all in trouble because of their wrong thinkin'. In any case, I didn't mean to be rude. Hunter says I need to be more polite. TomA says that, too. Be more social. And I probably shouldn't be saying out loud that I should be more social." She paused and then said. "How'd you sleep?"

"For the most part it was fine," he said. "But I heard that moaning and groaning again. Kind of unsettling."

Butch looked over at the house. She shook her head. "Don't know what that could be. Maybe later I'll check it out. When I get back. If you're still here."

"TomA invited me to stay," he said, "even though the visitors for the art spectacle will start arriving any time. Agica suggested I help her catalog and hang the art. I think I can manage that."

"I thought you were anxious to get back and get your son," Butch said.

"Of course I am," Mateo said. He sounded irritated. "But I can't be half a man if I'm going to fight. I have to be at my full strength. I want to be smart about this."

Butch nodded. "That is the wise thing to do," she said. "Unfortunately, I often don't do the wise thing. Or the smart thing. Like today. We're going to look for Jezebel. I should stay here and help with the ditch cleaning. But the sheriff thinks this cat is around, so I'll go look for her. Gotta be back before people start arriving for the Wayward Art Spectacle. Some shady characters show up. Don't get me wrong. It's fun, but they keep George and me on our toes."

"I don't really understand the thing with this jaguar," Mateo said. "I didn't know jaguars could live so long or have so much intent."

Butch shrugged. "The space time continuum being what it is

here," she said, "anything is possible."

Mateo looked at her. "I don't understand."

"It's not possible, and it's possible."

The back door to the Big House opened and George came through it, saddlebags hanging over each shoulder.

"Yapping or riding?" George asked. He shifted the saddlebags from his left shoulder and half-tossed it to Butch, who grabbed onto it. George kept walking toward the stables. Butch slung the saddlebags over her shoulder.

"I'd like to be eatin'," Butch said.

George reached into his shirt pocket, pulled something out, tossed it to Butch, and then kept on walking. Butch caught it.

"A boiled egg? A boiled egg is gonna help me track down a warm-blooded killer bent on my destruction? A warm-blooded apparently supernatural killer?"

Mateo laughed. Butch grinned. She tossed the egg to Mateo, who caught it.

"Peel this for me, will you, Bandito?" Butch said. "George is so irritable. Needs to get some—uh, needs to get laid. But then don't we all?"

Mateo cracked the egg on the table and then began peeling.

Butch turned back to see where George was and found a strange man standing a few feet from her. He was not very well dressed. Jeans dirty, shirt ripped. But he looked clean. Harmless, so she didn't reach for her guns, which she hadn't strapped on yet anyway.

"How the hell did you get here without Archie barking or someone else noticing?" Butch asked.

"Uh, I—Hunter let me in," the man said.

Herman Peterson. The Hermit. He didn't look quite as raggedy-ass as he had last time Butch had seen him.

"She's up now?" Butch asked. "I never seen that girl get up before eight her whole life."

"Are you going to interrogate him or give him a job?" She heard Hunter's voice behind her. She turned around as the girl came out of the house. Mateo held out the peeled egg to Butch. She took it. In two bites it was gone.

"Yeah, that's gonna hold me," she said. "I'm gonna interrogate him. That's what I do, girl." She turned back to Herman.

"I'm Herman Peterson," he said. "I can do all sorts of work. I'm good with horses. Hunter said you could use a hand with the ditch cleaning. I offer my services as a *peon de la acequia.*"

"That's up to TomA," Butch said. "He's the mayordomo."

Herman glanced at Hunter. Then he looked at his feet. Butch realized he had not looked her in the eye. She didn't give a shit whether someone looked her directly in the eyes or not, normally, if it wasn't part of their culture. If she got angry every time someone did something that didn't correlate with her particular upbringing and way of being in the world, she would be pissed off twenty-four hours a day, and she was too good-natured to be pissed off twenty-four hours a day. At least, she had ambitions to be good-natured all the time. Sometimes someone got on the wrong side of her and her Grandma No One nature kicked in, from breathing the same air as that crazy old woman all those years.

But this morning, with Hunter and Mateo watching every move she made, this morning, when she had not had anything to drink in twenty-four hours or more, she wasn't going to let Herman Peterson piss her off even though she knew it was part of his culture to look someone directly in the eye.

"This is what I need to know, Peterson," Butch said. "I know you've had some hard times. I know you've had some crazy times. And I can't let no one come here who might hurt anyone. Do you have your craziness under control?"

"It's not craziness, Butch," Hunter said. "It's a medical condition caused by—"

Butch looked at her. "Girl, if craziness ain't a medical condition I don't know what is," she said. "Now let me do my job. Unless you want me to send him packing?"

Hunter put up her hand and closed her mouth.

"Now, Mr. Hermit—"

"Herman Peterson," he said.

"What? Oh, yeah. Mr. Peterson, you think you can keep yourself under control, under lock and key as it were, and do the job or jobs assigned to you? Ditch cleaning is as old as the hills. Not as old as the mountains, but you get my drift. Generations of men have come together at this time of year, in an act of communal harmony. It's back-breaking work. I know. I did it a couple times, but there's always some superstitious asshole who thinks cuz there's a woman in the ditch, the weather's gonna be bad that year or all the cows are gonna dry up or drop dead or some horseshit. So then I'm supposed to go with the other women to cook and bring water out to the men, and the women are glad for that because who wants to stand in a ditch for hours on end doing back-breaking work anyway? But I ain't gonna cook and haul water, so George and I participate in the eatin' and drinkin' and celebratin' that the community will have water for another year. Not that George cares. Not his ditches, he says." She stopped talking.

Butch realized George was standing next to her and everyone was looking at her.

She cleared her throat. "Just giving a little history. Granted, most of it wasn't relevant to this conversation, so you might say it pisses me off a little bit. So I was saying, Herman Peterson, can you control your crazies?"

Herman looked at her. Then he said, without a hint of a smile, "I can do if you can do."

Butch's eyes narrowed. Hunter closed her eyes. George and Mateo may have stopped breathing.

Butch heard a hawk call out above them. She glanced up.

The hawk said, *"Home, home, home."*

Butch looked down again. Everyone was still looking at her, except Herman Peterson. He was staring up at the hawk.

Rosey whinnied. Herman looked back at Butch.

Butch smiled. "I like a man with a sense of humor," she said. "If TomA will take you, it's all right with me. No drinking, whoring, or swearing—"

"What?" Hunter said. "But you—"

"You didn't let me finish," Butch said. "No drinking, whoring, or swearing while you're on the job. What you do on your own time ain't nobody's business."

Butch glanced at Hunter. She smiled and mouthed the words "thank you." Then she went back into the house. Mateo got up, waved to Butch, and followed Hunter into the house.

"Butch, you gonna strap on so we can leave?" George said. "Half the day's over. Herman, you're good with horses I hear. I've got a colt you can look over while I'm gone. Let me show you."

"He'll be right there," Butch said.

George nodded. He took a hint better than most. He sauntered back toward the stables.

Herman looked down at his shoes again.

"Herman, I saw you heard the hawk," Butch said. "What'd she say to you?"

Herman looked at Butch again. "She wasn't talking to me," he said. "She was talking to you."

"But what did she say?"

"Didn't you hear her?" Herman asked.

"Yeah, but I want to know if we heard the same thing."

"I'm sure we didn't," he said. "Because I heard it with my ears and heart and you heard it with your ears and heart."

"First," Butch said, "I don't have a heart. Secondly, I like philosophers even less than crazy people."

Herman's face twitched slightly.

Apparently he didn't like being called a crazy person.

Butch growled under her breath. Sometimes being around people was too difficult. She had to watch every little thing she said.

"Sorry," Butch said. "Go on. See what mischief George has for you." She tried to sound cheery. But it really wasn't in her nature.

Herman walked toward the stables where George waited. George pointed to Butch and then pointed to the casita. Butch nodded.

TomA and Patrick came out of the house then and walked over to Butch. TomA embraced her. She gently pushed him away. Trick hugged her next. She pushed him away a little more forcefully.

"Don't try to pull me into your happy cult," Butch said as she stepped back from them. "What are you doing? Is this some new thing you've read about? Oh no, you've decided to try the heterosexual life, is that it? Well, boys, you're cute and everything, but I kind of think of you as my fathers so that would be repulsive."

Trick rolled his eyes. "Woman, can you be quiet for a moment? We heard about Angel. We were expressing our heartfelt distress on your behalf."

TomA nodded.

Butch made a noise.

"It ain't nuthin'," she said. "I'm sure it won't last."

"Merle T. Connolly," Trick said. "Ouch."

Butch couldn't argue with that.

"Yeah, that did sting," Butch said. "I guess she went with the exact opposite of me. Merle T. Connolly would be that."

"We're wondering if now is the best time to be running after

Jezebel," TomA said. "We know Sheriff Carter wanted you to see if she was around, but we're thinking it would be better if you stayed here. You always love the ditch cleaning celebrations. And you can stay and be a peon. I don't care. I'm not superstitious."

Butch shook her head. "I appreciate that," she said. "But I feel like getting out of town, being with some wild folk."

Patrick nodded. "We've noticed you've seemed out of sorts."

Butch gnawed on her lip to keep from saying anything. She was so fond of both men—although Trick got on her nerves sometimes—but she got uncomfortable when they were solicitous to her. She wanted to say, "Save it for the tenderhearted. I am rough-hearted."

"You didn't eat hardly anything last night," TomA said, "and we had to practically drag you into supper."

"And you didn't drink anything," Trick said. "That's not like you."

"You've been telling me for years I drink too much," Butch said. "So when I don't drink anything for a couple of days, you're panicked?"

"We're not panicked," TomA said. "We're not trying to intrude into your private affairs. We wanted you to know we're here if you need anything."

"Noted," Butch said. "Now George is gonna hang me if we don't get going."

"You won't change your mind?" TomA said.

"We might get back tonight," Butch said. "Who knows?"

She knew. She wasn't coming back tonight.

"By the way, I said Herman Peterson could work for you if you want," Butch said. "Hunter seems to have developed a kind of attachment to him. Not sure why. Gotta get my guns and such. See you in a few."

Butch hurried away from them and went into the casita. She breathed deeply as the door shut behind her. It was cool and peaceful inside. She looked around for her pistols. Where'd she put them?

She stopped and stood still.

What the fuck was wrong with her? She didn't hurry. She didn't need to. She always knew she would get to where she was going soon enough. And she didn't run away. Not from anything or anyone.

Mostly, she always knew exactly where her guns were.

She walked into her bedroom and picked up one from beside her bed. The other was hanging in the holster in the belt on the back of her door. She strapped on the gun belt and then put the left pistol into its holster.

She nodded.

Now all was right with the world.

She didn't need Angel. Angel was a nice respite from a cruel world.

Naw, she was just a nice respite.

She sighed as she imagined Angel's white skin and her golden hair brushing Butch's face as Angel leaned over to kiss her.

Butch shook herself. "Turning into a sentimental old woman," she said out loud. "Hope I don't end up pushing a broom in some dark hallway talking to assholes like me and George."

"Who you calling an asshole?"

Butch turned around. George was standing in the doorway.

"I didn't hear you," Butch said. "Close the door."

"You didn't hear me and you want to go out tracking a jaguar?" George opened his eyes wide. "Maybe we should delay this trip a bit."

"Sorry about the asshole remark," Butch said. "I'm feeling strange. Maybe this is why I drink in the first place. Or why I never stop. The world is a mighty strange place."

"Birds talking to you again?"

"More than that," Butch said. "TomA and Trick were commiserating with me about my love life. Like I'm some girl who needs her hand held. Me and Angel were just friends. Friends who had sex with one another. I can move on to someone else. No big deal."

"Then stop talking about it and let's hit the trail," George said.

"I been thinking a lot about Grandma No One," Butch said. "And stuff like that. I don't like thinking about none of it."

"If I said something like that to you, you'd say 'if you don't like doing something, stop doing it.'"

"Fuck," Butch said. "I hate when you quote me. I got no argument for that. Let's go track us some pussy."

George looked at her.

"Pussy cat, Mr. George," Butch said. "Get your mind right and quit imagining me naked."

"I don't need to imagine it," George said. "I've seen you naked enough times that it's been burned onto my retina."

"Lucky you."

"Keep telling yourself that."

"Asshole."

"Quit stalling," George said.

"They gone?"

"They all went back into the house," George said, "and Herman's out talking to the colt."

Butch nodded. "Let's do this thing."

Six

Butch and George headed out toward the acequia. It was a clear blue day. A soft breeze muted sounds, and the morning felt dreamy to Butch. She had to keep telling herself to stay alert as Rosey carried her through the desert.

They travelled to the area near the acequia where signs of Jezebel had been reported. Butch looked up into the aspens as they neared the ditch, in case Jezebel was waiting in a tree for them.

George and Butch dismounted their horses. George went in one direction, Butch in the other, both of them looking for sign: a footprint, claw marks on a tree or log, scat. Even smell. George could smell cat a mile off.

Butch crouched on the ground and stared at the reddish pink dirt and looked for prints. She saw deer, a smaller cat, and maybe fox prints. Nothing as big as a jaguar. And not Jezebel, who had a line through her left front paw from some kind of injury or birthmark.

No one had seen that scar print for years, even though several people claimed to have seen Jezebel. Butch figured Jezebel was dead.

Had to be.

The Jezebel stories had never been amusing to Butch, although the rest of the community seemed to like them. Every time she forgot about this sorry event in her history, someone would claim to see Jezebel. And when someone saw a jaguar, they immediately thought of Butch even though Jezebel had been around for as long as anyone could remember.

Some people believed Jezebel was supernatural. The Other People whispered that she was one of the People who had shifted into a jaguar and forgotten how to get back again.

Johnny Jack said he knew for a fact that Jezebel was actually the reincarnation of President William McKinley because he had died before his time.

When Butch—or someone else—pointed out that Jezebel had been living in the Blood Mountains long before McKinley lived and died, Johnny Jack shrugged and said, "Must be Abe Lincoln's reincarnation then."

No one listened much to Johnny Jack.

George had seen jaguars a couple times when he was growing up and then once when he was an adult. George did not believe in reincarnation. Or in shapeshifters. (Well, maybe he did, but he wouldn't let on.) Like Butch, he believed Jezebel was several different jaguars who lived and died and who had been spotted by various people over the years.

Butch had seen Jezebel a half dozen times in her lifetime, and it always looked like the same jaguar to her, the same jaguar who had supposedly been stalking her for half her life.

At least the fools who stayed indoors too often pickling their brains with alcohol believed Jezebel was stalking Butch.

In the early days, Butch had preferred to do her drinking outdoors like any civilized person.

And that was exactly what she had been doing when she first saw Jezebel.

94   KIM ANTIEAU

She and George had been up in a small canyon that the locals had nicknamed End of the Road Canyon, even though no road came down that way and the canyon wasn't much of a canyon. Butch was young, barely seventeen. It was not long before she almost burned down St. Anne's Home for Wayward Boys. It was a hot July day. Butch had been drinking some rot gut George had gotten from Merle T. Connelly.

Butch and George were trying to shoot a target George had set up against the cliff side. They only had one rifle so they shared it, tossing it back and forth between one another after they each took a shot.

At one point, George tossed the gun to Butch and said something about how Butch couldn't hit a target if it was painted on the ass of the biggest ass in the world. He thought that was funny, because he was drunk, and Butch thought he was laughing at her, because she was drunk, and she got pissed off. She went to shoot the target and she slipped. The gun went off, maybe the bullet hit a rock, or it ricocheted. Or maybe it didn't do any of that. George and Butch both ducked.

They were safe. The bullet missed them.

But everything got very still and silent.

It was so still that Butch and George looked at one another. Goosebumps popped up all over Butch's arms.

They listened to the silence.

"Something's wrong," George said.

"Ain't nothing wrong," Butch said. And then she said loudly to the canyon, "I grew up in Grandma No One's house. Nothing you got gonna scare me."

George walked over to the target and picked it up, along with his bag, and then he and Butch began walking. They didn't have any horses back then. Just their boots. Each held their gun up, ready, as though they were expecting an ambush. George had the rifle, Butch had an old revolver.

They climbed the ridge and ducked down to get under the pine trees, out of the sun.

Butch smelled something. Heard a cry. Someone weeping? Growling?

And then she saw something crumpled on the ground. Didn't look right. She realized then that something had stopped breathing only a moment ago. Something had been alive in this thicket, breathing as she and George laughed and shot off the rifle. Now it was no longer alive.

George swore and looked around. Butch got closer to whatever was on the ground. The orange color blended into the needles that softened the earth.

A jaguar cub lay on the needles. His eyes were open, not cloudy yet with death. One of the rosettes on his side was darker than all the rest. Blood. Butch put her hand on the cub's side.

He was warm. And dead.

"This just happened," she said.

"Yeah," George said. "It happened when you tripped and fell."

Butch stood. She took off her hat and put it across her chest. George did the same.

"May you find peace on your journey," George said.

They stood in silence for a few moments.

Then George looked at Butch. "If this was Jezebel's cub, she will kill us if she finds us here."

Butch heard a sound that made the hair on the back of her neck stand up. Later neither she or George could say what it was they heard. But they both turned around.

Ten feet from them, the mother jaguar stood watching them, her head down, her shoulders tensed. Butch had never seen anything so beautiful.

Butch knew the cat could take her head off in about ten seconds. Or less.

"It was an accident," Butch said. "I didn't mean any harm."

If you didn't mean any harm, why is my son dead?

Jezebel hunched down a bit more. Butch was certain she was about to leap when they heard a shot in the near distance. They all twitched, startled, and looked in the direction of the shot. Then Jezebel ran off. Or leapt away.

She disappeared.

"You want the hide?" George asked Butch when they were certain Jezebel was gone.

Butch shook her head. "You?"

"Naw."

They could hear someone riding up into the canyon.

They looked down at the cub. Butch had this strange urge to put her hands on the cat, see if she could make it live again. Something so awful about seeing this beautiful animal dead. For no good reason.

What would Grandma Crow have said to Butch if she had been alive? "You're done for now, girl." After all, jaguar was Butch's animal, at least one of them. Grandma Crow said everyone was born with a protector, and jaguar was Butch's protector. "So you can't ever, ever harm one."

Grandma Crow never told Butch what would happen if she did harm one.

The cub looked as though it had never been alive. Like Grandma Crow had looked a little while after she died.

George and Butch went back out of the woods and down the ridge again, hurrying away from whatever human was coming into the canyon. Hurrying away from whatever animal might be looking for them.

They didn't stay away. A short time later, they returned with a shovel. The cub was still there. George dug a shallow hole, and Butch gently picked up the animal and put it in the ground. She wasn't sure why she wanted to bury the cub. George thought it strange, said it was better to let the elements have it. But he sang for the cub anyway. They covered him up with dirt. Then they piled some stones on the grave and left.

After that day, Butch often had the sense that Jezebel was watching her. The townspeople thought the same thing. And when Butch had a couple of close calls with Jezebel after that, they all started talking about the cat that wanted revenge.

Butch never believed Jezebel wanted revenge. Animals weren't like that.

As Butch and George headed back home that day, back to Grandma Crow's house after they buried the cub, Butch had said, "Hey, George, what happens if you hurt your animal?"

"Jaguar is your animal?" George asked.

"That's what Grandma Crow said."

George was silent for a moment. Then he said, "Man, you better hope she was lying to you."

"Couldn't have been me killed that cub," Butch said. "Someone else musta been there."

George shrugged. "Maybe the cub killed himself." He laughed.

Now, as Butch looked in the red dirt for prints, she heard the rustle of leaves. She jumped up, pulled her pistol out, and aimed toward the noise.

No one was there. Just the wind moving through leaves left over from fall. Besides, if Jezebel came for her, Butch wouldn't hear her.

Not unless Jezebel wanted to make her presence known.

And that was a human trait. Jezebel was all wild.

So was her cub.

Butch holstered her pistol.

She could not have killed the cub. Not even by accident. She was certain of it.

Jezebel was not haunting her. Or hunting her.

Butch glanced over at the cottonwood trees. She saw a road runner looking at her.

She could almost swear the bird was grinning at her.

X marks the spot.

X marks the spot.

"Shit," Butch said. How could she have forgotten that?

"George, I done some bad things in my life," Butch said. "Mostly I don't regret them cuz I don't think about them. What can you do about something that's done? You can't undone it."

"Sometimes you can," George said, walking toward her.

Butch made a noise. "You're always contradicting me."

"Not always." He grinned.

"I was saying you can't undo the past in most cases. I can't make that cub live again. But I can clear my name. I can maybe find out the truth. If we dig up that cub, we can find the bullet that killed him, prove it wasn't mine."

"It's not a good idea to dig up the dead," George said.

"That's an obvious observation, George," Butch said. She whistled for Rosey who had wandered off in search of grazing. The horse trotted toward her. "Don't you have something more mystical to say? Or frightening?"

"Nope," George said. "That's it. I'm here to emphasize the obvious to you."

"Maybe it is time you got married," Butch said. "So you can annoy the hell out of someone else. George, don't you remember that when we went target practicing we only had one rifle, so I marked my bullets with an 'X' so we could tell ours apart when we pulled them out of the target. Dumb idea but we were kids."

George shrugged. "I don't see hide nor hair of Jezebel here. Might as well go dig up her kid and really piss her off."

"You're sounding like one of them," Butch said. "Crazy as hell."

"And you think it makes sense to dig up an animal that's been dead for a couple of decades so we can find the bullet that killed him?"

"Yes," Butch said. "I heard it in the Wind and the Wind never lies."

They stopped at Marigold Williamson's place, which was on the way, and borrowed a small shovel from her. She didn't ask them what it was for. She invited them in for a late breakfast. George declined the offer, but Butch accepted. She had always liked Marigold. She was a fine-looking woman with a good sense of humor and a way in the kitchen.

Marigold made them eggs, sausages, pancakes, and beans. They sat outside near a willow tree, in plain view of the horses and the mountains.

Butch had two helpings of everything. George, who had been reluctant to stop, also had two helpings.

"I like a woman with a good appetite," Marigold said. "You should come by more often, Butch."

"Marigold," Butch said, "don't tell Maria I said this because she would be mighty hurt, but this is about the best breakfast I have ever had in my life. How come a woman who looks as good as you and cooks as good as you never remarried? How come you're still single?"

"Same reason you are," she said. She squinted and looked up at the sky and then looked directly at Butch.

Butch leaned forward and cocked her head. "Is that so?"

"Sure," Marigold said. "I'm as ornery as you are."

Butch looked at George. He laughed out loud.

When they finished breakfast, Marigold walked with them to their horses. She handed George a bag with some biscuits in it. He stuffed it in his saddlebag, and then he got up on Bucket.

"Thank you again," Butch said as she got up on Rosey.

"I heard about that man found dead in the desert," Marigold said. "It's a shame."

"Yeah," Butch said.

"I hope this doesn't mean some murderer is on the loose." Marigold stood close to Rosey and looked up at Butch, shielding her eyes from the sun.

"Naw," Butch said. "I'm sure they'll figure it out. We're helping them some."

Marigold nodded. "I'm glad to hear that. By the way, Butch, I heard about Angel and Merle T. Connelly. Shame. He's such an asshole."

Butch laughed. "Won't argue with you there."

"And if you need any help getting over Angel," she said, "I wouldn't mind being that help."

Butch looked down at her. Marigold grinned. Then she turned and walked away, swinging her hips with a little more vigor than she had earlier.

"I might take you up on that," Butch called.

Butch laughed. Hell, maybe the day wasn't going to be all bad after all.

George and Butch rode their horses away from Marigold's place and up into the foothills of the Blood Mountains, the red mountains some people called the Blood of Christ Mountains. Butch did not understand that particular name for the mountains. They never reminded her of blood or of Christ. But then she loved these mountains and she was not particularly fond of those who worshipped Christ, at least not those who had run St. Anne's Home for Wayward Boys. When she was younger, she had wondered how St. Anne could be any kind of saint if she allowed places like the Home for Wayward Boys to exist. Of course, Butch had never heard of saints before she came to the home, and Sister Jeanmarie told her saints were exceptionally good people.

Sister Jeanmarie wasn't bad.

So perhaps not all the Christians were bad.

In any case, the mountains did not remind Butch of the blood of anything.

She loved the mountains because they were wild. Most times she didn't see another human being, besides George, while she was in the mountains. At a few spots, she could look down and see Santa Tierra. She had affection for the town, and she liked being up in the mountains, up as part of the sky, looking down at her town, imagining all the people safe and cozy, making love, eating, drinking, arguing.

Today they followed the switchback down into End of the Road Canyon. Butch hadn't been here in years. It seemed quiet and dull, the stone walls black and brown rather than red, the scrub still brown and blond from winter. Nothing green or colorful or new was coming up yet. The place still smelled of snow.

And something else.

The hair rose on the back of Butch's neck.

She listened. Heard the whine of some insect and ringing in her ears. Otherwise, it was desert quiet.

Rosey pranced restlessly. Bucket was quiet, but his ears twitched.

Butch took out her pistols and looked around.

"Cat?" George asked.

"I dunno," Butch said quietly.

Butch whistled.

She didn't hear anything, but something changed, shifted. Moved away? Rosey settled down.

George and Butch dismounted. They left the horses loose, in case Jezebel or any other predator was nearby. George got the small shovel from his saddlebag.

"We had the target here," Butch said, pointing to the canyon wall. "I shot and it ricocheted and went up there, we thought."

Butch moved her hand around until they were facing the ridge.

Butch could hear the shot again, in her memory.

Made her shiver.

Then the scream. Or death cry.

Couldn't have been a death cry. A jaguar cub wouldn't have made that much sound.

"That seems right," George said.

They climbed up the ridge, toward the pine trees, just as they had nearly twenty years earlier.

Once they were in the cool semi-darkness of the trees, they both glanced around.

"This does not look familiar," Butch said.

"Actually, it does look familiar," George said. "Like every other woods we've seen like this one."

Butch shook her head. "Yeah, a fine couple of trackers we are." She started walking around. "I remember there was a pile of rocks."

"Not a very big pile," George said.

They walked around the woods for a while. Butch tried to remember where they had seen the cub. The memory seemed so fresh in her mind, yet she couldn't tell exactly where she had originally found the dead cub.

She realized her heart was racing and her ears were ringing.

She stood still and took a deep breath.

"You got any booze on you?" she asked.

George looked at her. "No, you know I gave that shit up. Why?"

"I dunno," Butch said. "Lately I've been feeling strange. Thinkin' maybe it was because I hadn't had a drop to drink for a day or two. Might be messin' with my constitution."

"Could be," George said. "I remember this man once who

drank every day of his life, except when he was a boy, I suppose, and then he just stopped. Three days later he was dead. Body couldn't take it."

Butch looked at him. "It's been about three days," she said. "Great way to reassure me."

George made a noise. "The day you need reassurance is the day I hit the road."

"I might," Butch said. "You never know. I am a human being."

"Now you're messin' with me," George said.

Butch grinned. "Yeah, I can never fool you."

They both stood still and looked around. Butch breathed deeply. What would Grandma Crow say? She taught Butch to listen to the wind, the trees, the ground.

"Where are you, jaguar cub?" Butch whispered.

The wind shifted a bit. Butch smelled dust and something acrid, as though someone was burning something they shouldn't.

She suddenly remembered she had smelled something that day. Besides gun powder. Besides that sweet smell of blood.

Fresh wood. She had smelled fresh wood.

She closed her eyes. Breathed.

Yep, part of a tree had come down.

She opened her eyes and began walking again. She looked to her left and right. Some trees had broken branches, but she couldn't tell how long they had been broken.

Then she saw where a pine tree had been split in half by lightning. She strode toward it. The break was long ago healed. She remembered it now. They had originally found the cub not far from this broken tree.

Butch turned to her right. She saw blond grass coming up through a pile of rocks.

"George!" she called as she hurried toward the pile.

She looked carefully at the ground near the rocks and moved

the grass with her foot to make certain no rattler was hanging around. She knelt on the ground and began moving the stones to one side. When the stones were off the grave, George held out the shovel to her. Butch stood and took the shovel.

"Say a prayer to the spirits," Butch said.

George reached into his shirt pocket and took out a pinch of cornmeal. He whispered and released the cornmeal into the wind. The wind took some of it; the rest floated to the ground.

"I gotta clear my name," Butch said. "So I hope you'll forgive me, Jezebel."

Butch put the shovel blade on the ground, then used the sole of her boot to push the shovel into the coriander-colored dirt. She carefully moved the shovel down and then lifted the dirt and put it to the side.

"I don't think we buried him very deep," George said.

The wind picked up, blowing some of the dirt into Butch's face. The trees began rocking, moved by the wind or by some music Butch couldn't hear. Must be a storm brewing that they had not noticed on their way into the canyon.

Butch turned away from the wind and stuck the shovel in the ground again, moved another chunk of dirt. Then another.

Out of the blue, it seemed, the wind stopped. The woods were quiet.

Butch looked down. She could see bones.

Tiny yellow-white bones.

She tossed the shovel aside and knelt on the ground again. George squatted next to her. She slowly dusted the dirt off the bones with her hands.

There was the skull.

"Man, he was small," Butch said. "Hardly seems likely a ricochet bullet could have gotten him. I bet someone was aiming right at him. Couldn't have been me."

"Seem to remember he got shot in the side," George said.

Butch continued to carefully remove dirt from the bones. It was so dry, it wasn't difficult.

"There's his ribs," Butch said. She felt a lump in her throat. "Would have grown up to be a beautiful animal."

"Yeah," George said. "Until some rancher killed him."

Butch took off her jacket and laid it on the ground. Then she scooped up the dirt from the cub's chest cavity. She dumped the dirt on her jacket. Then she leaned over it and picked through the dirt.

No bullet. Some bone fragments.

She got another handful and dropped it on the jacket.

She picked through the dirt again. George leaned closer. Her fingers touched something hard. She held it up and looked at it.

Looked like a rock with dirt on it. Butch rubbed at the dirt. It fell away.

Underneath the dirt was a mushroomed bullet.

"Got any water?" Butch asked.

George shook his head.

Butch spit on the bullet, then wiped it on her trousers.

She held it up and looked at it.

"Can you see?" George asked. "Does it have the 'X'?"

"Too dark," Butch said. She started walking out of the woods. Then she looked back. "Can you make this right?"

"Sure," George said. "I'll fill it in."

Butch went out of the woods and stepped onto the edge of the ridge—and into sunshine. No clouds in sight. Must have been some kind of rogue wind they'd felt earlier. The sun was beginning to go down. Had they been in the trees that long?

She held the golden-silver bullet up close to her eyes. No "X" that she could see. She hoped she had been smart enough to scratch the "X" on the part of the bullet that wouldn't have splayed.

George came up beside her.

"I don't see any markings," Butch said. "I knew it couldn't have been me. I bet it was Merle T. Connelly. Remember, we saw him that day."

"What about under the metal here?" George said. "Where it mushroomed?"

"You think it could be under there? What are the odds?"

"You're probably right," George said.

Butch stared at the spent bullet. "Yeah. But I'd like to know. You got pliers or anything like?"

George gave her a look.

"Hey, you never know," Butch said. "You are a very handy man."

"Don't try to flatter me," George said. "Pueblo land is right over the rise. And Grandma Crow's place isn't far from that."

"Yeah, I know," Butch said. "It's gonna be dark soon. I'd rather not be tramping onto Grandma Crow's place in the dark."

"Still think her ghost is hanging around?"

"I never thought her ghost was hanging around," Butch said. "I lived there after she died. I lived there with you for years. I'd just rather get there in the daylight hours."

"You can lie to yourself but you can't lie to me."

"I lie to both of us all day long," Butch said. "But not the nights, baby. The nights I don't lie to you."

George laughed. "I bet you wish that bullshit worked on me."

"Naw, not really. It's a lot of work to try to be charming when it's not my nature. Let's get out of this canyon, make camp, and go in the morning."

Butch put the bullet in her shirt pocket. Then she and George went down the ridge together. The sun was nearly behind the opposite ridge. They'd probably have to stay in the canyon.

Wasn't smart to be wandering in the dark. Especially if Jezebel was around.

Better to stay in one spot so Jezebel wouldn't have to look for her.

Not that Jezebel was looking for her.

They bed down the horses, built a fire, and ate what Maria had packed in their saddlebags: burritos, boiled eggs, biscuits. They'd eat Marigold's biscuits in the morning.

"So Marigold gonna be your new Angel?" George asked as they lay on their bedrolls trying to sleep.

"Maybe," Butch said. "She seems willing. That's my first criterion." She chuckled. "See, you all thought I'd be different when I wasn't drinkin' so much. I'm pretty much the same."

George didn't say anything. The sky was clear, the stars bright. It was going to get cold. Butch hoped they'd gathered enough firewood.

"Maybe I'll go live with her," Butch said. "Spend my golden years out on her place, running off any varmints of the human kind. I gotta go somewhere if you're getting married."

"Because you don't want to live by yourself?" George said. "You could go live in the Big House any time you want."

Butch sighed. "Yeah, won't be the same. But you do what will make you happy."

Suddenly the hair on the back of Butch's neck stood up.

"What was that?" George sat up.

Butch looked out at the darkness beyond the horses. The horses had raised their heads, and their ears were twitching back and forth.

Silence.

And then a deep chesty roar.

Butch grabbed her revolvers and jumped up.

She had heard that particular sound once about ten years ago when she was out hunting what they thought was a rogue mountain lion; instead, they had stumbled upon a jaguar that the dogs had cornered on an overhang on a narrow ridge. The jaguar had looked directly into Butch's eyes. Butch had seen a spark of recognition in the animal's eyes. It was the same jaguar she had seen at the grave of the jaguar cub years earlier: Jezebel. The animal blinked then, as if to say, "We meet again."

The jaguar could have leapt for Butch. Probably could have killed her. Not without getting mauled by the hounds, but still. In any case, Jezebel had leaped into the air away from Butch and disappeared over the ridge

Butch had run up the ridge after her. When she reached the ridge, she saw a paw print, saw the line of the scar that was a characteristic of Jezebel's left front foot.

Now George was next to Butch. They moved the horses closer to the fire, and then they stood together, back to back, as they looked into the darkness, guns raised. George's back felt warm against Butch's, and the pistols felt strangely cold in her hands. The night tasted like mesquite.

"I told you we should not have fucked with the grave," George said. "In your entire life have you ever listened to me?"

"I listen to you," Butch said. "When you make sense. And maybe this time you had a point, except I don't happen to believe in immortal jaguars who are out to get me!"

"No one said she was immortal," George said, "just long-lived."

"Besides, she could have killed me twice now, and she didn't."

"Maybe she was biding her time," George said, "so that we'd be together and she could take us both out."

"Hell," Butch said, "we're together all the time. If she was that clever, she should have followed us after any one of our all-nighters at Angel's."

"Can we have this argument some other time?" George asked. "When some deranged animal isn't after us."

"I don't think it's the animal who is deranged," Butch said.

"McLean—"

"George, look at the god damn horses."

"Don't be using your white man religion to curse my horse," George said.

"I'm not a white man," Butch said, "and that ain't my religion. I'm trying to tell you that the horses seem perfectly calm. So unless they're in cahoots with Jezebel, she's gone."

They both dropped their arms—and their guns—to their sides. Butch peered into the darkness.

"Man, I need a drink," Butch said.

"I'll take the first watch," George said.

"We should have brought Archie," Butch said.

"Archie's older than Jezebel," George said. "We would have to carry him."

"Well, we need a hound dog," Butch said. She sat on her bed roll, then pulled it around her as she lay down. "I'm getting too old for this shit."

"Sweet dreams," George said.

"Shut the fuck up."

Butch fell right to sleep. This surprised her. Even in her dreams she was surprised. She was walking toward Angel's Heaven on Earth. She could almost taste the booze, could almost feel Angel's bare skin against her lips. The moon hung low in the sky, so low Butch felt like she could reach up and touch it. So she did. The moon slapped her hand away. Butch laughed. She heard the saloon doors swing open and then swing closed.

The squeak of them, the brief sound of laughter, and then the squeak again. A young woman hurried away from the door. No, wait, she was a girl. Fifteen? Dark hair, eyes shining blue in the moonlight, as though they were lit with a blue light from within.

"Suzanne," Butch whispered.

The girl rushed past her, didn't even look her way. The darkness ate her up, made a slurping sound as it swallowed her.

Butch ran after her, but a man blocked her way.

No, wait, he was a boy. Maybe sixteen? Fourteen.

Suzanne's brother.

She couldn't remember his name. Could never remember his name. Luke. John. Matthew.

Some religious name.

How come he was so blond when Suzanne was so dark?

The boy stared at Butch.

Suddenly she was under him, naked. Just like she had been all those years ago.

Only when he was done she could hear the other boys outside the room. Closet? They wanted in. She could hear them clamoring, shouting, breathing.

He reached for the door.

"If you let them in," Butch said, "I will tell them what you are."

Then she was running across the dark desert, still naked, her feet bare and bloody. She saw two lights ahead and ran toward them. They blinked on and off, on and off. She was almost there, almost safe, she could still hear the boys breathing behind her, mother fuckers, she would never let another one of them near her again, the lights blinked on and off, on and off, until she was at the source of the lights, saw the lights for what they were, as Jezebel sat in the desert waiting for her, her eyes beacons leading Butch to her. The jaguar opened her mouth and bared her teeth.

Butch gasped and sat up. She looked around. George was staring into the dying fire.

He glanced over at her. "You all right?"

Butch drew her knees up to her chest and rested her chin on them.

"Dreamed of Suzanne," Butch mumbled, "and then it was a memory, of the time I let her brother have sex with me." She groaned. "Stupid kid."

"Him or you?"

"Both of us," Butch said. "I had forgotten about the other boys. How they were all waiting to get in. How I had to knock out the window and crawl through it, run away in the darkness." She looked up and rubbed her face. "Man, George, I don't think this not drinkin' is working for me. I used to be a happy woman. Now I'm remembering shit I don't want to remember. I can barely stand my own company let alone anyone else's."

"Maybe the past is catching up with you," George said. "Maybe it wants an accounting."

"The past ain't a thing that would want anything," Butch said. "Just like Jezebel ain't immortal. Even though she was waiting for me in the desert when I ran away from those boys."

"In your dream or in real life?"

"What do you think?" Butch said.

"Hey, don't be biting my head off," George said. "I ain't your enemy."

Butch moved her head in a circle, trying to shake off the cobwebs of the dream.

"I know," Butch said. "I apologize. There aren't many things I regret in my life, but I regret that night."

"It got you outta that place," George said. "And we met."

Butch nodded. "Yeah, I guess. Funny how I went back to Wayward."

"Wasn't the same place by then."

"Lately," Butch said, "Wayward Ranch hasn't quite felt like home."

They were silent for a few minutes. Then George said, "You have *few* regrets? Should I remind you of a couple other things you might regret."

"No!" Butch said. "Go to sleep."

George lay back on his bedroll. In a couple of minutes Butch could hear his deep sleep-breathing. She peered into the night and looked for two lights blinking in the darkness. She figured Jezebel had to be out there somewhere.

Seven

Butch awakened at dawn. The ground was cold. She was cold. She glanced around. The horses stood quietly side by side. The sky was pale, drained of night and day. Looking at its colorlessness now, Butch wondered how it could ever achieve that preternatural blue she loved so much. The surrounding rocks and scrub were colorless, too, almost without dimension. She shuddered.

Twilight time at either end of the day was not her favorite time.

She kicked off her bed roll, then reached for her boots. She turned them upside down first, to make certain no critters had crawled inside. A few pebbles fell out. She pulled on the boots and then stood up and stretched.

Where was George?

Rosey looked over at her.

"Good morning, darlin'," Butch said.

"Come over here." George's voice.

"Where is here?"

George didn't answer. Butch walked around the horses and saw George looking down at the ground.

Butch went and stood next to George.

"Contemplating the universe in a single grain of sand again, George?"

He shook his head.

Butch followed his gaze. He was looking at a patch of sand, not much of it, just a piece of earth loosened into a bit of beach sand about the size of George's foot. Only there was an animal print in it.

Butch squatted.

It was a huge cat print with a line running through it, like the imprint of a scar or injury on the pad.

Jezebel's print.

"Just at the edge of the firelight," George said.

Butch stood. She shook her head. "I don't believe it," she said. "It's not her. Maybe it's a family trait, this line on the paw. Maybe one of her offspring was wandering by last night."

George nodded. "Yep. I like that explanation. Strange how she could have been wandering around here and the horses didn't raise a ruckus."

Butch kicked at the sand until the print was covered.

"Let's go," Butch said. "I want to prove once and for all that I did not kill that cub."

They snacked on leftover biscuits, and then they saddled the horses and headed toward Grandma Crow's place, the closest habitation between here and anywhere.

The ground got harder, rockier, and the earth and the rocks were creamy gold-colored rather than red. Trees seemed to disappear or shapeshift into scrub. And then Butch could see Grandma Crow's adobe house, barely distinguishable from the rest of the land. The wooden door was black and stood out from the rest of the house, like a painting on a wall. No one had lived in the house since George and Butch had left, except for the occasional vagrant. Butch wasn't sure why. Maybe because

Grandma Crow had died in the house.

Or maybe because Grandma *No One* had died there. At least that was what Butch had told everyone. Ten years old and she lied and said Grandma No One had gone to sleep that night and never woke up. It wasn't exactly true. Grandma No One had not been around for a long while before the night Grandma Crow died.

On that night, after Grandma Crow went to bed, Butch had awakened from a dead sleep, eyes wide open, sitting up in bed. She had listened to the night, listened to the darkness, and heard nothing except an owl screaming, trying to drive its prey out into the open on that dark moon night. Her heart was racing.

She didn't go check on Grandma Crow like she sometimes did when she awakened in the middle of the night. She didn't go outside and sing with the coyotes like she sometimes did. No, she felt the presence of Grandma No One in the house, and she wanted to hide somewhere, anywhere, but she didn't want to do anything to draw attention to herself. So she closed her eyes and made herself invisible. She made herself soundless, too, so Grandma No One wouldn't hear her breathing.

Then Butch heard the wind, only the wind was inside the house, not outside. She kept her eyes closed. Grandma Crow had warned her many times that what the white people called magic was just a part of Nature made visible, and most of the time it was meant to stay invisible. "Sometimes when you look at the Invisible, you are never right again. You've got one foot there and one foot here, one eye there, one eye here, one ear there, one ear here. Only crazy people look at the Invisible with both eyes wide open."

"Is that what happened to you?" Butch had asked her.

Grandma No One would have hit her for asking that question. But Grandma Crow nodded. "Yes. And only crazy people walk toward danger."

"So should I run toward danger?" Butch asked.

Grandma Crow laughed. "No," she said. "You never go looking for trouble. Otherwise you're creating a path so it can always find you."

That night, the night Grandma Crow died, a storm blew all around Butch, but she closed her eyes, closed her ears, and made herself fall to sleep.

In the morning, Grandma Crow was dead. Butch sometimes wondered if Grandma Crow had fought with Grandma No One that night. Maybe she had fought so long and hard against herself that she finally said, "This is enough. I won't let you hurt that girl ever again."

Butch didn't like the idea that Grandma Crow was dead, but she did like the idea that she had tried to protect Butch.

When the People asked her if it was Crow Woman or Grandma No One who had died, Butch started to say, "Grandma Crow died," but she didn't like answering this question. She didn't like that they asked such a thing. Didn't like that Grandma Crow had had to live so far from everyone because she was not like anyone else.

She also didn't like that the People had left Butch alone all those years with Grandma No One. Grandma No One could have killed Butch; no one would have ever known or cared.

Not that Grandma No One would have killed her. Butch never thought Grandma No One would hurt her so badly that she would die. No, it wasn't so much the beatings that bothered Butch—and they did bother Butch—it was the uncertainty of it all. Suddenly something would shift, and Butch could never pinpoint exactly what it was. Then Grandma Crow would disappear and Grandma No One would be there instead.

That wasn't exactly true. There was one pinpoint, there was one trigger, pivot point, whatever it was called. Grandma No One came when Grandma Crow drank. Not always, but often.

Grandma Crow didn't keep any alcohol in the house, but sometimes they had visitors. Someone would want to know why their cattle were dying or why so and so was cheating on them or when it would rain. And they always brought Grandma Crow liquor. She didn't drink it before she did any of her prophesying. It was always after the person left and she looked so tired, as though the life had drained right out of her. Then she had a taste of the liquor and slowly her color would return.

And so would Grandma No One.

Butch liked it best when they had no visitors.

Once or twice Butch made Grandma Crow something to eat right after the visitors left. She figured food was what Grandma Crow needed. Then she could get her energy back without the liquor and without Grandma No One.

It didn't work. Butch watched Grandma Crow shift into Grandma No One as she spooned Butch's soup into her mouth.

Butch didn't do much cooking after that.

Rosey whinnied and brought Butch back to the present. She patted Rosey's neck.

"There, there, girl," Butch said. She glanced over at George.

"Where'd you go?" he asked.

Butch shook her head. "Seems like lately I've been doing a lot of time traveling."

They pulled up the horses under the lone tall madrone near the house and then dismounted.

It was so still Butch could hear herself blinking, eyelashes meeting eyelashes.

For an instant. Butch felt like she couldn't move.

George was already walking into the house, had already opened the door.

A whoosh of air—or something else—came out of the house. George stepped aside. He shook his head.

"Maybe Grandma Crow was back for a visit."

He walked into the house. Butch was right behind him now. She barely looked around. She knew the place well, so there was no need. Bare adobe walls, dirt floor, window looking out at the mountains, the wooden table George had built and brought into the house. It was solid, sturdy, like George. He had carved flowers into the table legs.

George went in the back room and came out with some tools.

"Should take that toolbox back to the ranch," he said. "I'm surprised no one has stolen it yet."

"I'm not," Butch said. "This place scares most people."

"Good thing we're not most people," George said.

Butch picked the bullet out of her pocket and put it on the dusty table top.

"You want me to do it?" George asked.

Butch nodded.

George used the pliers to hold the bullet; then he hammered it. Or something. Butch wasn't sure how he was doing it. She didn't care.

She heard someone whimpering outside. She looked at George. He didn't look up from the bullet.

Butch walked to the door and stood on the threshold. The day was suddenly hot, the air shimmering, golden. She saw a girl walking toward the house. The whimpering came from her, Butch was certain, but she didn't look like she was crying. She looked angry. She was filthy. Her tears left streaks through the dust on her brown cheeks. Her black hair was ratty. Her dress was torn, her feet bare.

In the distance, behind the girl, a cat walked.

Butch squinted.

It was a jaguar.

Did the girl know what was behind her?

She knew she didn't know what was ahead of her.

She was pregnant. Very pregnant.

A boy ran out of the house. Butch stepped aside, but it didn't matter. He was made of light and memory, and he went right through her. He was tall and lanky. He looked so young.

George had always seemed old to her.

"Who sent you?" the girl demanded.

"I had a dream," the boy said. "An old crow came to me and said I should wait for you."

The girl sank to the ground.

Her feet were bloody.

"What happened to your shoes?" the boy asked.

"That's the question you ask me?" the girl asked. She began to cry. The tears washed the blood from her legs.

Then George was beside her with warm water. He gently washed her feet and then her legs. She wept in pain.

Butch couldn't believe she had ever been that young.

"Butch," George called to her from the house. She turned to look back inside. George held up the bullet.

She looked back outside.

The day was April cool again. The young George and Butch were gone.

Butch walked to George and held out her hand. He dropped the bullet on her palm. She picked it up and held it closer to her eyes.

There, where the metal had been bent and was now straight, Butch saw an "X."

All the air went out of her.

"Oh man," she said. She sat in the lone rickety chair next to the table. George leaned against the wall and crossed his arms.

"I never thought I did it," Butch said. "I couldn't believe I would ever harm something that beautiful. I'll never hear the end of it."

George laughed. "What do you mean you'll never hear the end of it?" he asked. "Everyone already thinks you did it."

"But I didn't," Butch said. "Fuck."

A wave of shame washed over her.

She suddenly felt like she was back at St. Anne's Home for Wayward Boys. Sister Claw was laughing at her and calling her a whore.

Not that Sister Claw had ever done that. She didn't laugh, for one thing. For another, she never called her any names.

Grandma No One called Butch's mother a whore.

Sister Claw didn't use names like that.

She demanded to know which boy Butch had seduced.

"I didn't seduce any of them," Butch said. "This was an immaculate conception."

Sister Claw hit Butch in the face.

"They all wanted to," Butch told Sister Claw. "They call me Bitch, you know. They think it's funny to change one letter of my name and make it into bitch. Sometimes they call me dog."

"Why do you think we named you Mary?" Sister Claw said. "We were trying to protect you."

"You weren't trying to protect me," Butch said. "You were trying to break me into kindling so you could burn me at the stake."

"That's nonsense," Sister Claw said.

Eventually Butch told Sister Claw who the boy was.

"Suzanne's brother."

"Who is Suzanne?" Sister Claw asked.

"The girl with the dark hair and blue eyes," Butch said. "She was here when the families visited. Twice."

Sister Claw's eyes narrowed again. For an instant, Sister Claw looked like Grandma No One.

Now Butch rubbed her eyes.

"You thinking about the boy?" George asked.

Since when did George wonder what she was thinking?

"What boy?" she asked.

George looked at her for a few seconds. Then he said, "The one you birthed."

Butch shook her head. "No, I don't think about him ever."

"I do," George said. "I think about him. I felt like he was our son, you know. He came from this place, eventually. Breathed his first breath here. He dropped into my hands. The women came here and put pollen on his forehead, held him up to the sun. He belonged here." George held his hands up to the sky.

"People don't belong to anywhere or to anyone," Butch said. "And he wasn't your son. You didn't fuck me in some broom closet."

George stared at her. Then he looked away and dropped his arms to his side.

"He was my son more than he was anyone else's," he said. "I would have laid claim to him."

"What is this?" Butch said. "Some kind of guilt trip? I gave him away so that he would not have to grow up in a shit hole like I did. So he wouldn't have to spend his childhood dodging someone's fists and dreaming about his momma hanging from a cottonwood tree."

"I wouldn't have let that happen," George said. "I would have taken care of us."

Butch shook her head. "I didn't want to be taken care of, George. I didn't want to be someone's mother or someone's wife. I could not have been a mother to that boy. Look at me. I shot and killed a baby jaguar. I drink too much. I fuck too much. I ain't nobody's mother."

"But I could have been somebody's father."

Butch nodded. "You still can be," she said. "Maybe you should go marry that woman." She looked at George. "Why are we having this conversation now?"

He shrugged. "We never talked about it before. Seems like some things get left unsaid too long they get rotten."

"So you been holding a grudge all these years that I gave the boy to Suzanne's mother?"

"Nope," George said. "Wasn't any of my business."

"George," Butch said.

He shook his head. Then he shrugged. "I can't explain it," he said. "When I held him in my hands, I felt instantly connected, as though we had been kin through space and time forever. I felt the same when I first saw you. I didn't feel that way about my own family. I always thought something was wrong with me. So did my family. And then I met you and then I met him."

"I remember you called him Zachary," Butch said. "I couldn't understand where you got that from. Couldn't you have come up with an Indian name? Zachary sounded so biblical."

"I don't know," he said. "I heard it somewhere and I liked it. We could have called him Zee for short."

Butch laughed. "Every kid wants to be named for a consonant."

"I've always wondered what happened to him," George said.

"They took him back East and he grew up," Butch said. "He's probably some rich guy now who would look down at the likes of us." Butch sighed. "Fuck. I need a drink."

She got up and went into the back room. Grandma Crow had lived in the lap of luxury: Her house had three rooms. Butch had spent her childhood sleeping on a cot in Grandma Crow's medicine room, where she dried and stored some of her herbs and foodstuff.

Butch went into that room, opened the toolbox, and lifted a bottle of whiskey out of it. She opened the top of the bottle and took a swig.

The warmth of the alcohol travelled down her throat, into her stomach, and outward through her arms and legs. She breathed deeply. Yep. That felt better.

She could put all this behind her now.

She took the bottle with her and went outside. George sat on the big rock beneath the madrone. Rosey and Bucket had their heads down, looking for something edible on the desert floor. Some bird Butch couldn't see and whose song she didn't recognize called out from the madrone. Butch smiled. Everything was so bright and clear. The small white flowers on this madrone looked like bells, and she was pretty certain she could hear them ringing.

"Are you ready to go back to town?" George said. "Sheriff Carter still wants our help."

"I'm staying here and looking for my mother's suicide note," Butch said. She took another swig of whiskey. And then another.

"Where do you think you haven't looked?" George said. "You've been looking for decades. The house isn't that big."

"Grandma Crow said when I was ready I would find it," Butch said. "I believe I'm ready. So I can find it." She looked out to where she had seen the jaguar following her younger self earlier in the day. She tossed the bottle of whisky to George and she walked south a bit, looking down at the ground as she went. No footprints from a pregnant fifteen-year-old.

But there on a nearly bare spot of ground were cat prints. And one of them had a line through them.

"Jezebel," Butch whispered.

"What are you looking for?" George was suddenly next to her.

She jumped, startled.

He followed her gaze.

"What is it?"

Butch looked at him. "Don't you see it?"

George shook his head. Butch looked down again.

She couldn't see the print.

She leaned over.

She blinked.

It was gone.

She stood up straight.

What was happening to her? Must be withdrawal from alcohol.

She needed more.

George shook his head. "What are we doing out here? We're supposed to be rescuing a woman or helping to find a killer. At the very least, the Spectacle is starting in a few days. We've got things to do."

"I don't believe any woman was kidnapped," Butch said. "Something about that story doesn't ring true. And we'll figure out what happened to Deputy Jones. No worries there."

"And what about Mateo Cruz?" George said. "Why is he still at the ranch? I thought he wanted to get his kid back, his kid who is in Mexico. Why are you covering for him? He probably killed Jones. It's ridiculous. What, you want to have sex with him first and then you'll turn him in?"

Butch rubbed her face. "What the fuck are you talking about? Cruz didn't kill that deputy. Yeah, something is fishy with his story but that ain't it. I don't want to have sex with him. I thought he was a good-looking young man, but that's not it. I felt protective. He lost his son, goddamn it. I can relate."

"You didn't lose your son," George said. "You gave him away."

Butch looked at George. She felt dizzy. Must be the booze.

"I'm going back to town," George said. "I've got stuff to do." He walked back toward Bucket.

"Gonna meet the new bride?"

"There's no water up here," George said. He tossed the bottle of whiskey back to her. "Rosey can't drink whiskey."

Butch stared at George. Was he actually telling her how to take care of her horse?

"You think you're talking to some tenderfoot?"

George took the reins in his hand and got up on Bucket.

"Hey, we learned you shot and killed a defenseless and rare jaguar cub," George said. "You were drunk then. You're getting drunk now. Who knows what could happen?"

Butch felt a rush of anger. She balled her free hand into a fist so she wouldn't reach for her gun.

She couldn't believe George was talking to her like this.

What had happened?

She let her fist relax.

"George," she said. "Why are you leaving me?"

He turned Bucket around and the horse started walking away.

"I'm not leaving you, Butch," he said. "I'm just leaving. Say hello to the ghosts for me."

Butch didn't watch him go. She headed back toward the house, taking another swig as she went.

She now knew the truth about the death of the jaguar cub. She was culpable. It was her fault. So wasn't it the right time to find her mother's suicide note? She needed it now. She needed some answers. Needed some truth.

Or at least a different truth. She didn't want the truth about the jaguar cub.

Or the truth about giving her son to that woman.

Whatever the truth was. The reality was that she had given her son away. It had been the right thing to do.

She didn't regret it.

She sat at the table.

She hadn't liked the woman. She had come to the house dressed in city clothes. Like she had stepped right out of some magazine advertisement about city folks and city clothes. She carried an umbrella or a parasol, or something to protect her face from the sun. Only it was black, and she was dressed in black—or purple.

A man helped her out of the carriage. Butch was holding the baby as the woman walked toward her. She had just nursed the boy. She hadn't known how to do that at first, had not really liked it, but she couldn't let him starve. And he was a cute enough baby, as babies went. He didn't cry much. He liked George's songs. He liked falling asleep next to Butch, even though she worried she would roll over on him.

The city woman walked toward them.

Butch asked what she wanted. Butch recognized her right away. She remembered her from family week, when the woman had come with her husband and daughter Suzanne.

Butch took another gulp of whiskey.

The city woman had said, "I am Elizabeth Endicott. I am to understand this boy is my grandchild."

The woman looked at the boy.

"He's so light-skinned," she had said.

"What's that supposed to mean?" Butch had asked.

"I thought he'd be darker," the woman said, "because you're Indian, right? Or Mexican? I thought he would be brown or black."

"He's the color of the land," Butch said. "When he was born I rubbed dirt all over him. Didn't you do that with your children?"

The woman stared at Butch.

"Why do you care what color he is?" Butch asked.

"This is probably the only grandchild Suzanne's brother will give us," Elizabeth Endicott said. Only she must have said her son's name.

"My family is wealthy," Elizabeth Endicott said. "My husband's family is wealthy. We know who our son is. We're grateful to you actually. Now we have an heir. We'll pay you whatever you want. We'll give you whatever you need. Let me raise the boy."

Only the woman hadn't said it all together like that. It seemed as though the woman stayed forever, trying to talk Butch into giving her her son.

"We can give him everything," the woman said.

"Then why is your son in that horrible place?" Butch said. "How do I know my son wouldn't end up the same way? St. Anne's Home for Wayward Boys is like a prison."

"We could make certain it is shut down," the woman said. "We'll take our boy home, too. We'll raise this child as our own. No one will ever know he isn't our son. You want more for him than this, don't you?"

Butch remembered looking over at the man in the carriage. She guessed if she didn't say yes to this transaction, the man would take the boy anyway. Maybe even hurt her and George. She thought about grabbing her gun, saw George eyeing his.

But in the end, she decided the woman was right.

She was fifteen years old. How could she take care of a child?

The woman tried to pay her.

"I'm not selling him to you," Butch said. "I am asking you to raise him as one of you, only better, so that he would never think of offering to buy a woman's child from her."

Not that she was a woman. She was still a girl.

A child.

"And his name is Zachary," Butch said. "You have to keep that name. If I track you down one day and I discover he's got a different name, I'll kick your ass. I know your name now. Elizabeth Endicott."

The woman looked frightened for a moment, as though contemplating a future where Butch would come knocking on her door.

Butch had held Zachary up so she could look into his eyes. Then she held him close to her. She loved the feel of his soft little body next to hers. She whispered in his ear, "Don't let anyone ever tell you your mother didn't care about you or didn't love you. You're a part of me forever. You're a part of George, too. You're a part of this place. And if you ever want to come home, you are welcome." She kissed his cheek.

She handed the baby to George and then she went into her room and got the tatters box. She opened it. She thought about giving the woman the cameo for Zachary, but that was more of a girl gift, she supposed. So she picked up the whistle. She put it up to her lips and kissed it. Then she brought it back into the main room.

She gave the whistle to the woman. "This was my mother's," Butch said. "I would like it to be his. I want him to know that if he ever needs anything, he can whistle for his friends. Maybe even for me."

The woman took the whistle.

Butch held out her hands for the baby. George kissed Zachary and handed him to Butch. George had tears streaming down his face.

Butch handed the baby to the woman.

Her fingers ached as she let go of him.

She picked up the bag by the chair. "Here's his diapers and rattle and such."

"I've got things for him," the woman said.

So she had known all along she would take him.

"Take it," Butch said.

The woman took the bag and the baby and began to walk away. Then she stopped and turned back.

"Are you certain I can't give you anything?"

"I told you," Butch said. "Call him Zachary, and treat him well."

The woman looked at her. Then she cradled the baby closer to her. The baby turned to look at Butch.

"I hope he is as fierce as his mother is one day," the woman said.

The baby held his hands out in Butch's direction.

Butch waved.

She heard Zachary giggle as the woman walked away with him.

Then he started to cry.

Butch went inside the house, went to the back room, covered her ears. She waited in silence.

Then she reached for the whiskey bottle and drank herself to sleep.

Her breasts hurt for weeks.

She never mentioned the baby again. To anyone.

George was sad for a long while.

Now Butch put her head on the table. She hoped the boy never thought she had deserted him. She didn't want him feeling the way she had about her mother. She had often wondered what she had done wrong, why her mother hadn't loved her enough to stay in this world.

Not that she spent a lot of time thinking about it.

But it haunted her.

That was why she wanted the suicide note. She wanted an answer. *Why, Momma?*

Except she didn't want to think about any of this.

That was not who she was.

Everyone had crap in their lives. The crap only hung on if people focused on it.

She wished she could go to Angel and rest her face between her breasts, listen to her heartbeat, feel her hands all over her.

She lifted her head, took another swig of whiskey, then got up and tore apart the house looking for the suicide note.

Again.

It was a tiny place. It shouldn't have taken that long, but Butch kept time-traveling. She tried to stop herself, but she kept going back to St. Anne's, or to this place with Grandma No One, or to the day she gave birth to Zachary. Dark Moon just before New Moon. Crows had begun to gather, first in the madrone, then on the house. They never said a word, they just came.

In the middle of the night she had contractions. She didn't know what they were; George had to tell her. How could anyone that young and that ignorant actually give birth to a real live child? George was steady, confident, but she could see the tears in his eyes, she knew the fear behind those eyes.

"The women should be here," he had said. He could have run to get them. Butch kept a hold of his hand and wouldn't let him. Maybe the Crow Women would have come down from the trees and the roof and the sky and helped her, if George had asked.

At one point, Butch fell to sleep or fell to death. She was standing on the riverbank. Her mother's body swung gently from the cottonwood. A child in a basket screamed. Butch went and looked at the child. She was going to reach for her when she saw a woman climbing out of her mother's body and dropping to the ground. The woman smiled and held out her hand to Butch. Butch reached for her, but Grandma Crow said, "No." And then Butch was back in the adobe house in the desert, giving birth to a baby boy.

"I heard one of the women say once that the mother has to go to the other side and bring the baby to this side," George had said. "I think you have to do that."

"I'm not a mother," Butch growled. "I want this over!"

"That's how it'll be over," George said.

"It'll never be over," Butch said. She closed her eyes. She reached back, beyond Grandma Crow, beyond the riverbank, she reached out to the stars, found her baby boy's hand, and she dragged him back with her.

"Not so fast, Momma," he said, "I'm coming!"

Then he dropped into George's hands. The sun was coming up. The women arrived and took the boy. They rubbed pollen on his forehead and showed him to the sun. George buried his placenta near the madrone.

Now Butch felt sick to her stomach. She was a good drinker. She didn't get sick. She didn't get ugly, either, as far as she knew.

Of course there was the time she shot and killed a jaguar cub.

Now she was sick and the sun had already gone down. It was dark.

She hadn't found her mother's suicide note.

She went outside, walked into the darkness, and threw up.

She felt something was watching her. Someone.

She stood and stared into the darkness. Everything suddenly seemed very clear. She no longer felt drunk. Or sad.

"All right," she said. "I will admit that I sometimes wonder what happened to my boy. There. Are you satisfied? Jezebel, I never meant to kill your baby boy. Here I am. If you want to exact your revenge, here I am. Of course, maybe you have already exacted your revenge since I spent this day in misery and loneliness. If you are responsible for this, good on you. But I'm done. I've got things to do. There may or may not be some woman missing in the desert. Some deputy got killed. And a strange man is looking for his son. Those things I can fix. I can't fix whatever did or didn't happen to me. I can't fix what I did to your cub. I can't fix the fact that I am talking to the darkness because I think there may or may not be a supernatural cat out there waiting to kill me. Oh wait, I can fix that. I'm leaving this place."

Butch went into the house again and put it back in order.

Then she saddled Rosey, mounted her, and set out into the darkness.

She could practically hear George saying, "That is a crazy ass thing to do."

"Rosey," Butch said, "I'm not feeling too well. But I don't want to be here any more. Take me home."

Clarity fuzzed up as soon as Butch got on the horse. It *was* a crazy ass thing she did. It was a stupid ass thing she did. Fortunately, Rosey was a super horse, by all accounts. She didn't ask for much, and she was more loyal than any person who ever lived. At least that was what Butch believed. Butch had raised her from a foal, after her mother was killed by a mountain lion, or a wolf, or a grizzly. Hell, Butch never knew what killed the mare. For all she knew, aliens did it. Farmers and ranchers always blamed something wild when one of their livestock died. By the time they found the mare's carcass, she was too far eaten through to tell what had killed her. To Butch's way of thinking, a grizzly, mountain lion, wolf or coyote would have gone after the foal, first, not the mare. The foal hadn't been touched. She was traumatized by whatever she had witnessed—or because she hadn't eaten in a while—but otherwise, she had been untouched.

Marigold's former husband was the farmer who brought Butch the foal who became Rosey. Actually he brought the foal to George because George was the horse healer. But Butch fell in love with her on sight. They had been together ever since.

The locals had stories about Rosey, just as they had stories about Jezebel. Some people swore they saw Rosey running around in the desert at night. Sometimes someone was riding her bareback—without a bridle or halter; sometimes she was racing around on her own or with another horse. When Butch heard these stories, she'd say, "Hey, what she does on her own time ain't no business of mine."

Rosey gave birth one year, and Butch had no idea who the father was. It wasn't Bucket. He'd had his balls sliced off years earlier. The foal—a filly—was the color of red rock. She never got accustomed to people, not even to George, and she ran off when she was a yearling, and no one had seen her since. The Irish in town said Rosey had obviously mated with the lost herd of Irish sea horses that supposedly ran through the Southwest, and Redrock was a result of that faery mating: She had just gone back to her own kind.

Butch appreciated the stories, but she didn't try to prove or disprove them. She sometimes wondered why people spent so much time making up stories about her life.

One day they'd probably make up a story about the night Rosey brought a drunk Butch through the desert safely.

Unless she fell off and died.

Or a mountain lion attacked them.

Or a jaguar.

Grizzly bear.

Star alien. Alien touristas.

Butch clutched the saddle horn and held on. Her ears were ringing so loudly she couldn't tell if those noises she heard were growls or belly laughs.

Finally she saw a light in the near distance.

"Rosey, go there," she said. "That looks homey."

She felt like she was going to be sick again as Rosey trotted toward the house. Butch knew this place, she was sure. Although through her drunken haze and the darkness, she didn't know where it was. Rosey whinnied.

Then the front door opened.

Marigold stepped out onto the porch. She held her shotgun

loosely in her hands. When she saw Butch, she set the gun down and leaned it against the house.

"Butch McLean, are you crazy?" Marigold asked. "It's pitch black out. What are you doing here?"

"I've come calling," Butch said.

Marigold stepped off the porch and came to Rosey's head.

"Lord, Butch, I can smell the stink on you from here," she said. "Go sleep it off in the bunkhouse."

She sounded angry.

"I'm sorry," Butch said. "I've had some bad news today. I didn't mean to come here like this. I saw the light, and it felt like a sign."

"A sign of what?"

Butch sighed. She couldn't think of anything clever to say. She couldn't think of anything at all. Except the truth, maybe.

"A sign that I should get my drunk ass self off this horse and seek shelter. I was pleased to see you, to see a friendly face, because I could sure use one."

"Are you too drunk to take care of Rosey?"

"I'm too something."

"Come on," Marigold said. "Let me help you down. You go inside, second door on the left down the hallway. You can sleep there. No throwing up. I'll see you in the morning."

Butch slid off of Rosey and into Marigold's arms. The woman was able to hold her up. Even in her drunkenness, Butch noticed and smiled.

Marigold pushed her away. "Go on. Sleep it off."

Butch stumbled into the house. "Second door on the left," she murmured. She turned, fell onto a bed, and that was all she knew.

Eight

Butch woke to the golden light of dawn. She turned away from it and saw Marigold, dressed only in a white camisole and white petticoats, leaning over the bed. Butch wanted to reach up and kiss the curve of her breasts exposed by the low-cut camisole.

Marigold smiled. "I was coming to get you for breakfast."

Butch sat up and looked around. She saw an open wardrobe filled with clothes, a chair with a dress draped over it, and a dressing table. "This is your bedroom?"

"Yes," Marigold said. "You don't follow directions well when you're drunk."

Butch looked down. She was naked, except for her camisole and short knickers.

"Did we sleep together?"

"Once I got the clothes off you," Marigold said, "the stink wasn't so bad."

"Did you have your way with me and I've forgotten the whole thing?"

Marigold laughed. "Honey, if I had had my way with you, you would not have forgotten, no matter how drunk you were."

Butch grinned. She reached for Marigold's hand, took it, and pulled her across the bed toward her.

"What about now?" Butch asked. "Do I stink too much now?"

Marigold laughed and lay on her back. Butch leaned over her and began kissing her breasts.

"I don't want to take advantage of you in your fragile state," Marigold said.

Butch looked at her. "Ain't nothing fragile about me," she said. "Least nothing that a little marigold wouldn't help."

"Well, then, I guess a bath and breakfast can wait."

Marigold and Butch made love until the sun was up and throwing golden light across Marigold's land. Then they had a bath—together—and breakfast.

Then they made love again.

At lunch, Butch said, "You sure know some fancy moves for some woman out all alone in the desert."

"Who says I'm alone?" Marigold said. "All kinds of creations pass by my house and come on in. You want more buckwheat pancakes?"

"Only if you've got more currants to go in them," Butch said. "I think you must be the best cook from here to anywhere."

Marigold got up from the table and went to the stove.

"That's only because you've seen me naked," Marigold said, "and because you don't cook. How can you go through life not knowing how to cook? Don't you feel kind of helpless, always waiting for someone else to make something for you?"

"I can cook enough to survive," Butch said. "What else do I need to know?"

"Besides how to find someone who will cook for you?"

Marigold poured the batter on the hot griddle. Butch pushed away from the table. Coffee cup in hand, she walked across the room and looked out the window. She watched the horses grazing in the field. Rosey seemed perfectly content. This was usually when Butch made her exit. She didn't like to stay around for food and small talk. Small talk usually led to some kind of criticism of her character. Like now. Like the fact she didn't cook.

"I ain't criticizing," Marigold said, "in case it sounded that way. I was curious how it was possible. I had to learn everything when I was a girl. How to shoot, cook, sew, slaughter an animal, hunt an animal, grow food, tame a wild horse. I figured most people had to learn the same things. Not knowing how to do one thing ain't nothing. I can't track the way you and George can. I can't get on with people that way you do."

Butch turned away from the window and looked at Marigold.

"You tryin' to charm me, woman?" Butch asked. "Tellin' me what I do well? You already got me into bed."

Marigold laughed. "Sit down and eat these."

She put the pancakes on a platter and carried them over to the table. She and Butch sat down next to each other.

"I don't get on with that many people," Butch said. She lifted two pancakes off the pile and put them on her plate. Then she poured maple syrup over them. "In fact, I try to avoid people."

"That's not true," Marigold said. "Everyone in town knows that if they're in trouble, they can count on you. You know how to figure things out. I admire that. I can barely figure out my own life. But you seem to understand the way things work."

Butch took several bites of pancake and was silent while she chewed.

Then she said, "I never thought of it that way. I never thought about it period. I take care of Wayward Ranch, so I sometimes take care of other things so that we can have peace and harmony on the ranch. I figure that's the least I can do after all they've done for me. Plus they pay me."

"Do you know who killed that deputy, or whatever he was?"

Butch shook her head. "No, I got a little sidetracked. Lately I've been thinking about the past. It's got me all mixed up. I'm not the contemplative type, in case you didn't know."

"You're very observant, though," Marigold said. "I've always noticed that about you."

"Yep, that's what it is," Butch said. "I notice when things aren't quite right. When things are a little off. I had to when I was a kid—pick up on the subtlest of clues that Grandma No One was about to make an appearance."

"I heard tales about your grandma when I was a kid," Marigold said. "A couple of times I'd see you and Grandma Crow, and you looked like two peas in a pod."

"Grandma Crow was good to me," Butch said. "She wasn't my real grandma, though. My mother was some whore who hanged herself down by the creek. Jane McLean."

Marigold shook her head. "I never heard about that," she said. "Surprised I didn't."

Butch shrugged. "I don't think folks talked much about some prostitute who done herself in. Grandma Crow happened by and she took me in. None of the white folks did that, so I owed her. Anyway, I notice little things, even when I can't quite explain what I'm noticing. And now there's a lot going on, Miss Marigold."

"I want to hear all about it," Marigold said.

Butch looked at her, took a breath, and then she told her everything: about Mateo Cruz, the jaguar corpse, finding the bullet, going to Grandma Crow's place. And then she went all the way back and told her about getting pregnant, about walking to Grandma Crow's and George coming out to help her.

"I never told anyone all of that before," Butch said.

"No one knows about it?" Marigold asked.

"George knows," Butch said, "because he was there. Elizabeth Endicott knows, and her boy, the one who had sex with me. The nuns know, but I don't know where they are, and I don't know if they know I eventually gave the kid to the Endicott woman."

"I'm honored you shared this with me," Marigold said. "I won't tell anyone."

Butch shrugged. "I ain't ashamed. It doesn't have much to do with me now." She paused. "Except that I keep thinking about it. George says he thinks about it a lot."

"This explains you and George," Marigold said.

"What do you mean?"

"He loves you," Marigold said. "Fiercely. Everyone knows it. No one would fuck with you because you're you, but also no one would fuck with you because George would kill them. Not figuratively either."

"Sure, we love each other," Butch said. "We're like brother and sister."

Marigold shook her head. "I think he loves you more like a husband loves a wife."

"Naw," Butch said, "although we have a running joke about that. He'll tell me he is secretly madly in love with me."

"Maybe it's not a joke."

"Of course it is," Butch said. "He fucks more women than I do."

Marigold raised her eyebrows. "I feel so special now."

"I didn't mean it like that," Butch said.

Marigold laughed. "I'm only playing with ya. Come on, Butch. I'm an independent woman. I can take care of myself. Remember, I killed my husband and buried him in the back pasture when he wouldn't do as I asked."

Butch looked at her. Marigold looked back.

"Not really," Butch said.

"Jesus," Marigold said. "No! I gave him a divorce. I only married him to have babies and that didn't happen, so he wanted out. I said I would give him the divorce as long as he didn't ask for any property. This land belonged to my ancestors, and I didn't want anyone else getting it, unless they were kin. He's living in California now with some dancer from San Francisco."

"I'm glad it wasn't the other thing," Butch said. "I'd have to report you to the sheriff, you know. I could probably never have sex with you again cuz I'd be a little nervous that you might get pissed at me."

"Aren't you glad it wasn't the other thing then?" Marigold smiled. Butch leaned over and kissed her.

"I better get going," Butch said. "You hear if the ditch cleaning went well?"

"I think it's about done," Marigold said, "and all is well in our little kingdom. Let me know what you find out about everything. I want to hear the rest of the story."

"You're coming to the Wayward Art Spectacle, aren't you?"

"Sure, every year," Marigold said.

Butch kissed Marigold good-bye again, and then she went out and whistled for Rosey. Soon Rosey was saddled up, and they were headed toward town.

Butch stopped Rosey in the desert near to where she had bumped into Mateo Cruz that night. She got off the horse and walked the area, crouching here and there to look at the ground. She looked around until she saw the stake and the flag Sheriff Carter had told her he had planted where the man had fallen. She walked over to it. The ground was nearly black, in a circle, where the deputy had presumably bled to death. Butch shook her head. It was a shame.

She glanced up, squinted, and then looked across the desert, past the scrub and the occasional cholla, to the cottonwood and other deciduous trees in the near distance that blocked any houses from her view. She turned in a circle as she gazed.

"Could have been anyone standing anywhere," she said.

She looked down at the circle of blood. She took off her hat and put it across her chest. "Rest in peace, brother," she said.

She walked back toward Rosey who stood watching her, near the spot where Mateo and Butch had first met. Butch suddenly realized she had been gone for days. For all she knew, Mateo Cruz could have left town, or maybe the sheriff had arrested him.

Rosey whinnied.

"I'm coming," Butch said.

A breeze washed across Butch's face and the sun glinted off a piece of something on the ground near a lone agave plant. Butch walked over to the agave and bent down so that her face was almost touching the blue-green leaf blades. In the dirt near the plant was a broken metal chain with a pendant on it.

Butch lifted the chain and the pendant out of the dirt.

The pendant was a "B" with a flower blooming from the bottom of it.

Just like the "B" on her cameo, the one she kept in her tatters box.

"What the hell?"

Had it been in the desert forever or had Mateo Cruz lost it the other night?

Butch dropped the chain and pendant into her breast pocket, mounted Rosey again, and continued into town. The dusty sloping streets were busier than usual, with fancy carriages parked here and there. An occasional automobile went by. Butch hated those things. They were noisy and they stunk up a place for hours. This time of year the town had to tolerate all kinds of intrusions that were considered good for business. Folks came from all over for the Wayward Art Spectacle.

Butch didn't mind it much. She usually had fun with someone pretty or someone passionate. She wasn't fussy.

She saw Deputy Fargo and Deputy Paper outside Molly's Restaurant, eating together. Seemed Fargo wasn't so worried about the kidnapped woman that he couldn't take some time for lunch.

Or maybe they had found her while Butch was gone.

Martin Paper looked up as Butch and Rosey moseyed on by.

"You find that woman?" Butch asked, without stopping.

"Not a trace," Fargo said. "Heard there are some strangers at your place though. Might come out later and check 'em out."

Butch shook her head. "We've got lots of strangers at Wayward now. It's Spectacle time. Better fill him in, Paper."

She didn't see any sign of Bucket, so George must be at Wayward. She glanced at Angel's Heaven on Earth as she and Rosey went by the saloon. Butterflies flitted in her stomach.

She would miss Angel. Probably in a few weeks or months, she'd be able to return to the saloon and they could be friends.

Unless Angel actually married Merle T. Connelly.

Butch shuddered.

She wasn't ever gonna get used to that.

Maybe she'd start hanging out at O'Henry's. Too many artists and intellectuals went there, but they were better company—sometimes—than the bunch of degenerates that frequented Angel's.

Butch stopped at Agica's house and dismounted Rosey. Aggie mostly lived upstairs. The front of the house was used as the historical museum and library. Butch went up on the porch, knocked on the front door, then went inside.

"Aggie, you here?"

"In the back," Agica called.

Butch walked down the hall to the large back parlor. Agica was sitting at her desk.

"It's a beautiful day," Butch said. She sat on the sofa across from Agica and looked around the room. Every wall was filled with shelves filled with books. Next to Agica's small wooden desk were several cabinets. Butch knew the cabinet drawers were stuffed—neatly—with historical papers. Agica knew more about the history of the place than most anyone else. Generally speaking, Butch knew very little about the history of Santa Tierra. When she was younger, she had wanted to find out about her mother, but Agica had never found a record of a Jane McLean. Butch figured they didn't keep records of the lives and deaths of prostitutes.

"Just a few things I had to catch up with before I get out to Wayward today," Agica said. "We've got the whole show hung. It's really fantastic. We missed you at the ditch cleaning festivities. Everything all right?"

"All is well in my world," Butch said. "But I was wondering if you still have the records from St. Anne's Home for Wayward Boys? I want to see the list of students who were living there about the time I left. I think it was the last year they were open."

"Sure," Agica said. She didn't ask any questions. That was one of the things Butch appreciated about Agica She wasn't intrusive. She was always finding out things for people, and she kept it all to herself.

Agica got up, went to one of the cabinets, dug around in one of the drawers, then pulled out a stack of papers. She took them to her desk and flipped through them.

"The nuns were meticulous record keepers," Agica said. "Here's the list. I don't see you on it."

"I wasn't a student," Butch said. "I was a prisoner."

Agica held out a piece of paper to Butch. Butch took it. At

the top of the ledger sheet was the name A. Barranco; at the bottom was Ernest Walters. Butch scanned the in-between names. There was one Endicott. Matthew Endicott.

"This guy, Matthew Endicott," Butch said, "do you think you could track him down? Or his mother, Elizabeth Endicott? They were from Boston. Pretty rich. I think they sent the kid out here to cure him of his hankerings."

Agica looked at her and raised an eyebrow. "Elizabeth and Matthew Endicott?"

"The kid may be a junior," Butch said. "Had a sister, Suzanne. He seemed kind of weasely, but Suzanne was a looker."

"Elizabeth and Matthew Endicott?"

"Yeah, why do you keep saying it?" Butch said. "I need to get a hold of the mother."

"Butch," Agica said. "These people are a very well-known Boston family."

"Are you saying I could write to them in care of Boston and they'd get my letter?"

"Uh, well, um, I can try to find out how to reach them," she said. "You know, you could probably telephone them."

Butch shook her head. "Naw. I think a letter would be better. I'll threaten to come out and track them down if they don't answer." She smiled. She liked that idea. She looked at Agica. "I'll tell you sometime." She stood. "Oh, I wanted to show you this." She pulled the broken chain and pendant out of her pocket and held it out to Agica. "You ever seen anything like this before?"

Agica came around the desk and looked at it. "You mean a pendant like this? I've seen them. Made out of metal. Pretty fine work. I've never seen a 'B' quite like this before. Where'd you find it?"

"It was in the desert, not far from where the deputy was gunned down," Butch said. "And I have a cameo, in my tatters box, that looks a lot like this. I wondered if it meant anything."

"Maybe it's a family heirloom?"

"Or maybe it's something some passing trader was selling cheap," Butch said.

Agica shrugged. "It's difficult to say. Sorry I can't help."

"It's nothing," Butch said. She put the chain and pendant back into her shirt pocket. She was going to have to talk to Mateo Cruz about this—and a few other things. Something was not right. "Better get home. We've got a Spectacle to protect."

"You all right?" Agica asked.

Butch nodded. "Sure. Just strange days, these days, you know?"

"Yes," she said. "Saw Angel today."

"And?"

"Remember I told you things keep coming up missing?" Agica said. Butch nodded. "It happened to Angel. She had these tiny silver pistols—they didn't work; they were some kind of keepsake."

Butch knew what they were. She had given them to Angel after she won them in a poker game from some dude from Los Angeles who claimed they were made from pure silver. They looked like a miniature pair of Butch's non-silver pistols. She was surprised Angel still had them. Angel never seemed to like them, or anything that had anything to do with guns. Actually, she didn't seem to like anything about Butch. Except being naked with her.

"Next time you see her," Agica said, "you might want to ask her about it."

Butch shrugged. "I'm not seeing Angel much these days. Did you ask her about it?"

Agica smiled. "That's not what I do, Butch. That's what you do. I asked her when she had last seen them. She didn't know. I asked her if anyone seemed particularly interested in them. I didn't know what else to ask. I'm not the one who fixes things around here."

"Sure you are," Butch said. "You're going to find those Endicott people for me."

Agica watched her.

"I'll go talk with Angel," Butch said. "But I don't know how I'm going to track down someone who is stealing worthless pieces of junk."

"My father's inkwell wasn't junk."

"But an old dog collar? Some crappy silver pistols that don't even work. I've got other stuff going on, Aggie."

"You are in a mood," Agica said. "I'm only keeping you apprised about what's going on in town, so you can head off trouble at the pass. Just doing what I've always done. You don't want to know this stuff, I won't tell it to you."

"Awww, Aggie, calm down. I'll see what I can do."

"Don't tell me to calm down," Agica said. "You ever think maybe you should either stay drunk or don't drink at all? Because this in-between moody stuff ain't fun for the rest of us."

Butch put her hands up.

"Okay, okay. I'm trying to get back my easy amiable ways, but they seem to have flown the coop. And if you're steering me toward Angel because you think that will make me feel better, it's a lost cause. I ain't going anywhere Merle T. Connelly has been. At least not willingly."

Agica looked down at her pile of papers. "I'm only the messenger. Do what you want."

"I'll see you soon."

Butch left Agica's place shaking her head. She wasn't in a "mood," but Aggie sure was. Who cared about someone stealing a bunch of junk?

Butch patted Rosey on the rump, and then she walked across the street and down a bit to Angel's Heaven on Earth. She didn't hesitate. She walked through the swinging doors, paused a moment until her eyes adjusted, and then strode to the bar where Angel stood washing glasses in her empty saloon.

Butch walked over to Angel and stood across the bar from her.

She was as pretty as ever.

"You've got the stink of another woman on you," Angel said.

"You've got the stink of a man on you," Butch said. "What's your point?"

Angel shrugged and didn't say anything.

One of her golden curls barely touched the curve of her right breast.

"Aggie said you had something stolen and thought I should talk to you about it."

"It was those pistols you got me," she said.

"They ain't worth nuthin'," Butch said. "Why are you fussing about them?"

"They had sentimental value to me."

"I can look for them, but I have my doubts that I'll ever find them."

"Because you took them?"

Butch squinted. Was that what this was about?

"Me? Thievin' ain't in my blood," Butch said. "Even for something that was once mine."

"Well, there were some bullets on the nightstand, loose like, and they got stole at the same time."

"Bullets? You never let guns into the bedroom," Butch said.

"They were Merle's if you must know," she said. "He was counting them or doing something before he went out hunting. The next morning they were gone, along with the pistols."

"Maybe the thief thought the bullets would work in those tiny pistols," Butch said. "I didn't steal Merle's damn bullets and I can't believe you'd think that. I've got better things to do than this. Have a happy life, *chica.*"

Butch turned around and strode across the room. Her cheeks burned. She felt mightily pissed off.

Where was a tequila bottle when she needed it?

No, no, she was just getting over one hangover.

"Wait, Butch," Angel said. "I didn't really think you stole them, but I had to be sure."

Butch stopped. She took a deep breath and then turned around again, but she stayed where she was and looked at Angel, standing across the room behind the bar in semi-darkness.

"They remind me of you," Angel said. "So I didn't want to lose them."

"You don't need no reminders of our time together when you're a married woman."

"I know," Angel said. "It's not a good idea, but you know, I've always been filled with bad ideas." She smiled, and Butch's stomach lurched.

"Anyone out of the ordinary hanging around?" Butch asked. She took a couple of steps forward. Then stopped again.

Angel shook her head. "No, not really. Same old people. And I mean old. I had that Hermit guy in a couple of times cleaning up and stuff. A day or two ago."

Butch sighed. "I told you you shouldn't hire him."

"I heard you'd hired him on at Wayward and I figured it was all right for me to have him then."

Butch should have never let Hunter guilt her into hiring the man.

"He told me he actually had a room in the house," Angel said. "I figured it would be okay."

"Let me see what I can find out." Butch started to leave again.

"You're not staying?" Angel asked.

Butch looked over at Angel. Her head was cocked to one side and she ran her finger along the bust line of her dress.

"Merle's out of town," she said. "And no one's here."

Butch groaned. "It's tempting," she said. "But I don't think I should be exploring any land where Merle T. Connelly has already planted his flag."

Angel's face instantly changed. She picked up a glass and threw it at Butch. Butch ducked. The glass hit the wall and shattered. Butch laughed.

"See you later, darlin'!" Butch said as she walked out of Angel's Heaven on Earth. She glanced up at the sign as she started walking toward Rosey. "I guess it's all hell on Earth for me from now on."

Nine

Butch rode Rosey back to Wayward. She passed other riders and carriages on the road to the ranch. The gates were open, and her quiet home was now bustling with activity. She recognized many of the men and women, some of them area artists, some of them townspeople come to help, gawk, or bring food and supplies. Wayward Art Spectacle didn't officially start for two more days, but it was like this every year. The Spectacle started early and went on for days.

She saw Hunter outside the house with Jimmy and Maria. Butch nodded "hello." She did not want to be the one to tell Hunter that the Hermit was most likely thieving.

As Butch rode toward the barn, she felt like a stranger in her own home. Where was George? Mateo? Patrick and TomA stood close to the barn, talking with Alden Adams—negotiating with him more likely. Every year he created amazingly life-like sculptures that he put around the ranch, and every year he fussed and threatened to take them elsewhere. Right now, the three of them stood next to a wolf sculpture. The wolf looked completely realistic—except for her bright blue fur. The three of them waved genially as Butch rode by them.

Butch rode Rosey right into the barn—which wasn't anything she normally did. Bad luck, you might say, but she wanted to get away from the crush of people. She dismounted and then unsaddled Rosey, who seemed to watch her pensively.

"Rosey, I'm getting tired of going out and tilting at windmills," Butch said. "How about you? Everyone wants us to save them, but it's usually about saving themselves from themselves. Angel wants me back but she wants to have babies and be married. She doesn't know how to live with her choices. I tell you what, darlin', I know how to live with my choices. There's regret sometimes, but that's life. People are mad at me now because I don't have more regrets. This is who I am. Maybe I drink too much. I can work on that. Maybe I talk too much sometimes, but that don't hurt nobody. Maybe I've got me one too many women in one too many ports." Rosey stared at her. "Okay, so now is one of those times I'm talkin' too much. I'm just stallin'. I've got to go accuse Hunter's friend of stealing."

Butch sponged off Rosey, curried her, then put her out into the pasture. By the time she was finished, some of the seeming chaos outside had calmed. Some of the visitors had left. Butch glanced around but didn't see the Hermit. She had to stop calling him that. His name was Herman Peterson. *Herman Peterson.*

She saw Mateo Cruz under the trees talking to TomA. They both looked over at her as she walked toward them.

"So you're still here," Butch said when she got to them.

"And you're here again," Mateo said.

"Good to see you, Butch," TomA said. "We were starting to get worried about you."

"How'd the ditch cleaning go?"

"It was great," TomA said. "Especially the celebrations. I've never been to such an auspicious dance."

Butch didn't ask what he meant by that because TomA loved

any kind of celebration and every one of them was the best he had ever attended.

"It went so well and we had so much help we finished our part of it earlier than usual," TomA said. "We've just been getting work hung and set up. Patrick and Aggie have been doing a stellar job as usual. But I better go see what's up. George is out checking the property, making certain nothing is afoul, I suppose."

TomA walked away from them. Mateo Cruz smiled at Butch. Butch had so much to ask him.

"Have you been sleeping in the house still?" Butch asked.

"Yes," Mateo said. "I guess they didn't have as many overnight visitors as they thought they would have, so I'm staying put for now."

"Any more strange noises in the night?"

"You mean have I heard any more crying and screaming?" he asked. "Actually, I have. Every night, almost like clockwork. Only wakes me up for a moment."

Butch nodded. "I need to figure something out and then I need to talk with you more. Has the sheriff or anyone been out to the ranch asking about you?"

Mateo looked momentarily frightened, and then he said, "No, why?"

"Nothing," Butch said. "I want to make certain. I'll talk with you soon."

She excused herself and went up the steps and into the Big House. It felt like ages since she'd been here. Maria stood over the stove stirring something in a pot.

"Brewing up trouble, eh, Maria?" Butch asked. She went over to her and kissed her on the cheek.

"Where you been?" Maria said. "We all missed you. It's not the same here without you."

"Ahhh, I bet none of you noticed anything."

"I did," Maria said. "I've had too much food left over lately. But then your appetite isn't what it once was."

"That's over," Butch said. "I was trippin' down memory lane, and it wasn't fun."

Maria looked over at her. Butch held her gaze for a moment.

She had almost forgotten that Maria had known about her pregnancy and baby. Maria had begged the nuns not to send her away when they found out she was pregnant.

"I tried to stop them," Maria said.

Butch shrugged. "It's the past," she said. "It doesn't matter now."

"I went after you," Maria said, "but you disappeared. It was as though the desert made you instantly its own, and you were camouflaged. Or something." She shook her head. "I never knew. Worried you were dead until you came back here a couple years later."

"I was glad to be out of here," Butch said. "It was a freakin' battle every day. I look around sometimes and wonder how the hell I ended back here, but it was never the place, not really. It was the people. And they all got theirs. At least I hope so. Hey, Maria, what about this Herman Peterson. How's he been doing?"

Maria nodded. "He's good," she said. "He follows direction very well. He needs direction right now or else he doesn't know what to do. He left the hutch open and one of the rabbits got out and got killed—well, we figure its dead because it's gone—and he was very upset about that. But he's good in the kitchen and he's good with the horses."

"Notice anything missing, I mean since he's been here?"

"No," Maria said. "He's not a thief. He just needs some love and kindness, just like you did when you first came here."

Butch rolled her eyes. "You're comparing him to me?"

"You both came from war zones," she said. "Of a kind. You both were wounded and needed a home."

Butch made a noise. "I'm not wounded," Butch said.

"I didn't say you were wounded now," Maria said.

"You know he's staying here, don't you?" Butch leaned against the stove and crossed her arms across her chest.

"I don't know what you mean," Maria said. "Isn't he staying in the bunkhouse?"

Butch laughed. She pushed herself away from the stove and left the kitchen. She walked down the hall, went across the Big Room—where she barely noticed the new paintings or Patrick who was talking with one of the artists—and then she hurried up the stairs. At the top, she went down the hall to the room the nuns used to lock her into. The door should be locked (or stuck) now.

She put her hand on the doorknob and turned.

The door opened easily.

The single bed was made, although the blanket was a bit crooked. At the end of the bed were several items. Butch reluctantly stepped inside the room. Even though she had been able to get out of the room each time the nuns locked her in, she was not fond of it or this floor. They had intended it to be her prison and it still felt like that.

On the bed was an old dog collar and a broken doll.

So Herman was the thief.

For what purpose would he take these things?

"Don't be mad."

Butch turned around at the sound of Hunter's voice.

Strangely enough, she wasn't mad.

She did feel a little hurt.

"You lied to me," Butch said. "You snuck him up here and said he could stay here, only he couldn't let me or TomA find out."

"Yes, that's true," Hunter said. "Although I didn't actually lie to you."

Butch made a face.

"Okay, omission is a lie," Hunter said. "But you hated him so much."

"I didn't hate him," Butch said. "I don't hate anyone." Maybe Sister Claw and some of the boys from the school. But that was so long ago; maybe she didn't hate them any more. "I didn't trust him. I lived with a crazy woman if you remember, and I didn't want a crazy person living in this house so close to you all. Mateo says he screams and cries half the night."

"Mateo told you he was here?" Hunter asked.

"No, I figured it out," Butch said. "You sleeping with him?"

"No!" Hunter said. "It's nothing like that. I thought he needed sanctuary and you weren't going to give it to him. Sometimes you can be really mean, and you were mean about him."

"I can be mean? But I'm so good-natured."

"Not all the time," Hunter said. "Sometimes you are a mean drunk."

"What?" Butch said. "If that's true, why didn't anyone tell me this before?"

"Why is it our responsibility to tell you you're being an asshole?" Hunter asked. "You always taught me that I had to be responsible for myself. You're not always a mean drunk. Just sometimes. I try to avoid you then."

"Well, fuck me," Butch said. She leaned her head back and closed her eyes. Had she become Grandma No One?

"Did I ever hurt you?" Butch asked.

"No," Hunter said. "As far as I know you never hurt anyone physically. You just got mean, especially to George, and probably to the person you were sleeping with at the time."

Butch felt her face burning.

How could she not know this?

She cleared her throat and looked down at the bed.

She picked up the dog collar. "Why is he stealing stuff like this?"

"I didn't know he was," Hunter said. "But can we ask him nice without accusing him?"

"Sure, darlin'," Butch said. "You go ask him whatever you like and then get back with me. Some of those things he took— or may have taken—have sentimental value for folks. They might want them back."

Butch stepped out of the room. Hunter moved out of her way, and she closed the door.

Hunter put her hand on Butch's arm.

"It's all right," Hunter said. "You didn't mean any harm. You're a good person."

Butch frowned. Then she put her arms around the girl and embraced her.

"You don't have to take care of me, darlin'. If I did wrong, I need to own up to it. Maybe my drinkin' days need to be over."

"But then you get sad, don't you?"

Butch stepped away from Hunter and looked down at her.

"You know a lot for being a kid," Butch said.

"I ain't a kid," Hunter said. She pointed to her breasts, one at a time. "See, I got these. You said once I got these and my blood, I was a woman, and I needed to act like one."

"Which meant what?"

They walked down the stairs together with their arms around each other's waists.

"Which meant I could be whoever I wanted to be and do whatever I wanted to do. That's what you always said. 'Don't let anyone define you. You're undefinable.'"

Butch laughed. "I'm not sure that makes any sense, but if it worked for you."

"You know I think of you as my mother," Hunter said. "I got two dads and I've got you."

"Oh man," Butch said, "then you're in trouble."

When they reached the Big Room, Butch slapped Hunter on the rear. "Now get going and find out what mysterious thing the Hermit—I mean, *Herman*—is doing."

"Will do."

Hunter ran ahead of her, down the hall. Butch felt like she had to sit down. She almost felt like she was going to cry.

"You okay, Butch?" Patrick asked. He was up on a step ladder trying to hang a painting.

Butch looked over at him. He smiled. He and TomA had been so good to her.

She shook her head. "I—I'm fine. Thank you kindly for asking, Patrick. You need some help there?"

"Bob and I can do it," Patrick said. "You go get yourself something to eat. You're looking a little peaked."

"I'll do that."

Butch went down the hall and through the kitchen. She walked out the door without a look at Maria. She felt shame, and she didn't want to talk to anyone. She was a mean drunk? She had always figured she was a fun drunk.

She looked around for Mateo. George believed he was the kidnapper and bank robber. Maybe he was right. Butch lifted the pendant and chain out of her pocket where it rested next to the bullet that had killed the jaguar cub. What if Mateo had been lying about everything?

She spotted Mateo over by the barn. She dropped the pendant back into her pocket and motioned Mateo over to her as she walked toward the casita. When he got to her, Butch opened the door to the casita and they went inside.

"George?" Butch called.

No answer. The place was empty. And clutter-free. George

must have picked up. She needed to do that more often.

"Sit here," Butch said. She motioned to the table and chairs. George had made this table and chairs too. Just like he had made the table at Grandma Crow's house.

Butch glanced around the room. Wasn't much to it. Cupboards. Sink. Small wood stove. No pictures. No paintings. Just like Grandma Crow's place. Empty. As though no one lived here.

Butch closed her eyes for a moment. Then she shook herself and went into her room. She picked up the tatters box and opened it. She pulled out the "B" cameo, then went to close the box and put it on the stool, only it slipped out of her hands and dropped to the floor. The contents spilled out.

"Crap," she said.

She bent over and picked everything up and put it back in the box and then set it back on the stool.

She went into the kitchen and sat at the table with Mateo, who was watching her every move.

"I think you've been lying to me about everything," Butch said. "I can't help you if you don't tell me the truth."

Mateo swallowed.

So Butch was right: He was lying about everything.

Butch took the pendant out of her pocket and laid it on the wooden table top.

"This yours?"

Mateo looked at it. He smiled. "Yes!" He picked it up.

"What is it? The 'B,' I mean."

"It's a family heirloom," Mateo said.

Butch stared at him. Then she shook her head. "Everything that comes out of your mouth is a lie. If you don't start being honest with me, I'm gonna run you off, and it won't be pretty."

"I stole it from my uncle," he said. "My uncle Hector de la Baranco. I don't know why. I just did it. Where'd you find it?"

"I found it near where the sheriff was shot and killed," Butch said. "Did you kill him?"

"I didn't," Mateo said. He leaned forward. "I have not killed anyone. I have not shot at anyone. I have not kidnapped anyone. That is the truth."

"Why are you really here?" Butch asked.

Mateo looked at his hands. "If I told you, you wouldn't let me stay."

"I'm not going to let you stay if you don't tell me."

"There's no ex-husband," he said. "It's my uncle who has my son. He says I'm not responsible enough to raise him. My uncle is coming here for the Wayward Art Spectacle. Something about this town he likes so he comes every few years. Now that my son is four years old, he thought he would enjoy the Spectacle. That's why I came up here. My uncle always stays at the Fremont Hotel when he visits, so I want to go there and take my son from him. And I want your help."

"You want me to help kidnap your son?"

"It wouldn't be kidnapping," he said. "He belongs with me. I have enough money. I can make a life for us."

"Because you robbed that bank?"

Mateo nodded. "Yes, yes, I did that. I didn't hurt anyone."

"What about the woman?"

"There was no woman!" Mateo said. "I dressed up as a woman. I knew they'd never suspect a female bank robber."

Butch shook her head. She didn't know what to do, or what to say.

"Please," Mateo said. "I just want my son back. Just because my uncle is rich doesn't mean he has a right to take him from me."

"Are you telling me everything?"

Mateo didn't say anything for a moment. He set the pendant back down on the table.

"This pendant isn't actually a family heirloom," he said. "I stole it because I wanted to hurt my uncle. He's raised me since I was—since I was young, after my parents died. I don't know exactly what the 'B' stands for—it's not the family symbol, or the family name. It's something to do with his first wife. I don't know her name, but she died a long time ago. She killed their little girl and then hung herself. Right here in this town, I think."

Suddenly everything shifted for Butch. Time stood still or raced forward. Butch thought she heard a cat roar. Or maybe it was a mouse. Her vision narrowed. Her legs got wobbly. She could barely speak.

"What?" Butch said.

Mateo nodded. "It was quite tragic. They never found the child's body. She was four years old, I think, or younger. It broke his heart. He was never the same after. But that's no excuse for how he treated me."

Butch pushed away from the table. She picked up the pendant and stuffed it into her pocket, along with the cameo.

"Butch, what's wrong?"

"I've got to go," she said. "I—I'll try to help you with your son. I'll be back."

Butch could barely see, or think. She tried not to run, but she rushed out of the casita and to the barn. She couldn't help it: She ran to the barn. She whistled for Rosey. Her trusty stead galloped over to her. Butch put on her bridle, the saddle blanket, and the saddle. She tried to adjust the belly strap but her hands were shaking.

"You all right?" Hunter came up behind her.

Butch breathed deeply. Then she said, "I had some startling news. Having some trouble with this."

But then she did it. She tested the strap to make certain the saddle was secure.

"Did you find Herman?"

"Not yet," Hunter said. "Jimmy and I are going to go look for him. Thank you for not blowing up."

Butch got up on Rosey. "Me? Blow up? Naw. If you see George, could you tell him I'm going to the Fremont Hotel? I could use his help, I think."

"Sure," Hunter said. "Be careful."

"Always."

Rosey and Butch galloped away from Wayward.

Butch tried not to think about anything on the way to town. It could mean nothing. It could mean something.

She rode up to the hotel and let the stable boy from the Fremont take Rosey. The horse was hot and lathered up. Butch kissed Rosey on the nose. "Take care of her," she said, and then she let the horse go and she went into the Fremont.

She took off her hat and went to the registration desk.

"I need to speak with Hector de la Baranco," Butch said. She didn't know the clerk. He looked at her skeptically. Fortunately Larry Fremont came by then.

"Larry," Butch said quietly, "I need to have a private conversation with Mr. Baranco. Now."

Larry nodded. He was known to be the most discreet man in town.

"He's in suite 204. Top of the stairs and turn left."

"Thank you, Larry. I owe you."

Butch took the stairs two at a time. When she reached the top of them, she turned left and walked down the hall until she got to room 204. She knocked.

She heard a deep accented voice say, "Come."

She hesitated, breathed deeply, then opened the door.

The room was huge and lavishly decorated in red and black velvet. Or something. Butch couldn't be sure. She still could barely see or concentrate. Her heart was racing.

Sitting at a desk across the room was a man with black hair going gray. He looked up at her and smiled. He had black eyes. Something about him seemed familiar.

Ah yes. He looked like Mateo.

He stood and came toward her. He wasn't very tall, but he was trim and good-looking.

"I'm sorry," he said. "I thought you were room service. May I help you with something?"

"Are you Hector de la Baranco?"

"I am."

"I—I'm working with the sheriff," Butch said. "I'm Butch McLean. We're trying to track down a killer and a bank robber."

"I'm so sorry," he said. "How may I help? Please sit."

Butch sat on a hard cushioned chair across from a sofa that the man sat on as soon as she was seated.

She felt like apologizing for her appearance and her dirty clothes.

Not that she thought she should be in a dress.

She just wished she was . . . cleaner.

"Do you know a Mateo Cruz?" she asked.

He shook his head. He still smiled. How congenial he seemed.

Butch wondered where Mateo's son was.

"Do you have someone here with you?" she asked.

He frowned a bit. He looked confused. Then he said, "Why, yes, I do. In the other room. My grandson. He's with his—how do you say, his *niñera?* His nanny.*"

His grandson?

Butch took out the pendant and held it out to him.

"Does this belong to you?"

He got up and took it from her.

"Yes! Where did you find this! It means a great deal to me. I thought my daughter had taken it when she ran away."

"Your daughter?"

"Yes, I'm sorry," he said. "It's a sad family drama I won't bore you with."

Was his daughter the kidnapped woman? So Mateo had lied about that, too?

Butch pulled the cameo from her pocket and held it out to him.

"Does this mean anything to you?"

Hector again stood and looked at what was in Butch's palm. He gently took it from her and then sat on the couch. He suddenly looked much older.

"Where did you get this?" He stared at the cameo.

"It was my mother's," she said. "It was in a keepsake box next to her body. She left it there, along with me, when she hung herself."

"Your mother?" he looked up at her.

"Jane Sarah McLean," Butch said.

The man's eyes watered.

"Sarah Jane McShane Baranco," he said. "She was my wife."

Butch shook her head. "No, my mother was a whore who hung herself after the father of her child deserted her."

Hector shook his head. He stood and looked down at her. She got up so that they were standing at eye to eye.

"Do you have a birthmark on your left shoulder?" he asked. "Shaped like a rose?"

Butch blinked. She breathed. "I do."

"My little AnnaBella," he whispered. He put his arms around Butch and held her tightly. Butch didn't know what to do.

She pulled away.

"Is this some kind of flimflam?" she asked, stepping back from him. "Are you and Mateo in cahoots? Lots of people have seen my birthmark. Lots of people know my mother's name was Jane Sarah. I don't have a dime. So I can't imagine what you want from me. My mother was a prostitute who hung herself because the man she loved was going to marry someone else. It's an old story, cliché almost."

"No, no," he said. "I don't understand any of this. Sarah Jane was a teacher here. She was beautiful. She looked just like you except she had red hair and blue eyes. We met when I was here on a business trip. We fell in love. My parents had arranged a marriage for me, but I wanted to marry Sarah Jane. Unfortunately she got pregnant before we were married, so the magistrate married us. We planned on getting married in the church later. She stayed here with you—with AnnaBella—and I went back and forth. My parents disowned and disinherited me. I kept going back, trying to reason with them, trying to pave the way so that Sarah Jane, you, and I could go back home. But Sarah Jane was depressed after you were born and she never quite recovered, probably because my parents would send their emissaries when I was away to try to bribe her or berate her, telling her that she had ruined my life. It was difficult. I was trying to find a way to make a living. Then I went away to visit my parents and I was gone longer than I thought I would be. I wrote to her, but I never heard from her. Then I got a message that she had hung herself and drowned the child."

Butch shook her head. "It's a coincidence. It can't be the same person."

"It was 1883, about this time of the year," he said. "She hung herself from a cottonwood tree down by the creek. She had a box of keepsakes, some letters were in it, along with this cameo. I never found the box."

The tatters box?

"It can't be the same," Butch said. "My mother killed herself in 1882."

"Are you sure?"

"That's what my grandmother told me."

Grandma No One, who lied about everything.

"Your grandmother?"

"The woman who found me at the creek near where my mother died. She took me home and raised me."

Hector backed up and sat on the sofa. He put his head in his hands. Then he looked up at her.

"I had that cameo made for your mother," he said. "I had the pendant made for me. It was to celebrate your birth. I gave the cameo to your mother on your first birthday. It would be our gift to you on your eighteenth birthday. We named you after her mother Anna and my grandmother Bella, the mystic of the family. We nicknamed you Bella."

Now Butch had to sit down.

"I used to imagine that the 'B' stood for 'beautiful,'" Butch said. "I knew it couldn't have stood for 'Butch.' I mean who would name their kid after a butcher?"

Hector stared at her. "Are you a ghost?"

"I don't think so."

"But how is it possible?" he said. "They said you were dead."

"That means I can't be AnnaBella. I am alive. And Grandma Crow said she tried to find my relatives. Seems like someone would have claimed me."

He shook his head. "I don't understand. They never found AnnaBella's poor little body. I always imagined animals had eaten her, and that has given me nightmares for decades."

Butch and Agica had looked through town records for any information on a prostitute who had killed herself. But they had been looking for Jane Sarah McLean who died in 1882, not a teacher named Sarah Jane McShane Baranco with a child who had died in 1883.

"I have the same birthmark," Hector said. "The star, on my left shoulder. Would you like to see it?"

Butch looked at him. He wasn't a flimflam artist. He was no scoundrel. He looked like a man in agony.

Butch shook her head. He stood and held out his hand to her. She reached up and took his hand and stood across from him.

"Your mother loved you more than anything," he said. "And so did I. So do I. This is a blessing, a miracle." He embraced her again. She didn't know what to do, so she patted his back.

Then she gently pulled away.

"I'm so sorry I didn't find you," he said. "I didn't know. They told me you were dead."

Butch's legs felt rubbery. She wished George were there.

"I—I don't blame you," she said. In fact, she had never given her father a second thought. She figured he had been one of her mother's many customers.

"You're saying my mother wasn't a prostitute?"

"No, of course not!" he said. "She was a good and virtuous woman."

They sat on the couch next to one another.

"She wasn't crazy religious, was she?" Butch asked. "I can't stand crazy religious people."

He smiled. His smile wavered.

"No," he said, shaking his head. "She worshipped god in the desert, in the plants, the ground, the sky. She heard god's voice in the wind, in a bird's song. But she couldn't shake her melancholy. She thought for certain I would desert her and you and she would be homeless, since she couldn't make her living as a teacher any longer. She had been such a strong and sure woman."

"Are you saying I sapped the life out of her?"

Hector looked at Butch. "Not at all," he said. "You were the one part of her life that cheered her."

"I didn't cheer her enough to keep her from killing herself."

"You must remember she had to have been very ill to do something like that."

"Why did you leave her alone?" Butch asked. "If she was so sick."

"I didn't understand the extent of her melancholy," he said. "It has haunted me all the days of my life."

"Didn't she have any family she could turn to?"

"Her parents were elderly," he said, "and they lived back East. She had a sister. I wrote to her when Sarah Jane died, but I never heard back from her. She didn't live far from here, if I remember right."

"Did you marry the woman your parents wanted you to marry?" Butch asked. "After my mother—after Sarah Jane—died."

"No!" he said. "I didn't speak to my parents for many years. When my father died, I inherited his land and business. My mother welcomed me back home. Then I remarried. Adriana was born soon after."

"I have a sister," Butch said. She looked over at the man who was her father, the man sitting next to her on the sofa.

"This is so strange," she said. "Why are you here now?"

"I wanted to take Frederico to the Wayward Art Spectacle," he said. "I have always loved it here, ever since your mother and I lived here. I had intended to go with my daughter, too, but she ran away from home. After the bank was robbed, I thought she had been kidnapped. I was desperate. I paid the deputies extra to find her. But now I hope they don't find her."

"Why?"

"Because now I believe my daughter was the one who robbed that bank," he said.

"I thought she was forced to rob it by her kidnapper," Butch said. "Or something like that. Although Mateo Cruz swears he didn't kidnap her. He claims you have his son. He says he's your nephew."

Hector shook his head. "No, I have no nephew called Mateo Cruz. Adriana has always liked to dressed as a man. I believe she pretended to be a man to rob that bank. I didn't know what to do. I'd been waiting at home for news of her, but I couldn't stay still any longer. Adriana knew I had been planning on coming to the Wayward Art Spectacle. So I thought we should come in case she decided she wanted to contact me. The deputy is trying so hard to find her because of the money I paid him, and once he does, he'll know she's the bank robber. I don't think even I could keep Adriana out of jail if she robbed a bank. And now one of the deputies has been killed. I can't believe Adriana would ever harm anyone. But what if she is now a killer, too? The deputy was just here and fortunately for Adriana, they have no leads."

Shit.

How could Butch not have figured this out?

She was supposed to be the sharp one, the astute one, the person who could tell when things were out of balance.

That was why Mateo Cruz looked so young, was so slight. Butch made a noise. No wonder Cruz had known the plot of *Jane Eyre.* It was because Mateo Cruz was Adriana de la Baranco. *Her sister.*

The bank robber.

"I know where your daughter is," Butch said.

"You do?" he asked.

"Yes, and she did rob the bank," Butch said. "There is no Mateo Cruz. She wasn't kidnapped by anyone. She came here with the intention of taking her son and running away to live some place in the United States. Why have you kept Frederico from her? He is her son?"

"She was acting irrationally," he said. "She was drinking

and staying out all hours of the day and night. She wouldn't marry the man we found for her. Now I'm afraid she'll never marry. She will be considered a fallen woman, a pariah. Her mother is bereft."

Her mother. Ahh, yes. Butch shook her head. She couldn't wrap her mind around any of this. She had a father, then a sister, then a nephew, and now a stepmother?

"Essentially you're keeping her son from her because she won't marry the man you want her to marry?" Butch said. "Isn't that a double standard. Or at least ironic? Although, truthfully, I never really understood irony."

Hector nodded and then shook his head. He seemed as confused as she was.

"I—I was trying to make Adriana's life better," he said. "In our culture, she needs to have a man in her life if she has a child."

Butch shrugged. "It's not right to keep her from her son. Set her up here, or nearby. Up here we don't care so much about those things."

That wasn't completely true.

"I suppose I was too harsh," he said. "I had lost one daughter. I didn't want to lose another. Adriana has always been headstrong."

"What the hell does that mean?" Butch asked. "The nuns used to say that about me. Maybe Adriana wants to be whoever she wants to be instead of some cultural stereotype. You got to be who you wanted to be. Let her do the same."

Hector looked at Butch. "I wanted to be husband to Sarah Jane and father to AnnaBella."

"So you're going to punish Adriana because your dreams didn't come true?"

"No, that's not what I meant. She acts without thinking sometimes."

"I'll give you that," Butch said. "Wasn't the smartest thing to rob a bank. Or to plot to kidnap her own son from you." Butch sighed. How could she fix this? Hector couldn't now pay Deputy Fargo to go away; his partner had been killed.

Hopefully Butch's sister was not the assassin.

Her sister.

"Can you take me to her?" Hector asked.

Butch shook her head.

"Not yet. I think I've got a plan to fix this. Meet me at the sheriff's office in two hours. Bring your grandson. And just go along with whatever I say."

He nodded. "All right."

Butch stood and put out her right hand. "It was a pleasure meeting you, sir," she said.

He stood and shook her hand.

"You can call me *papá,*" he said.

"Ah, maybe, eventually," she said. "Gotta go."

She quickly left the room and went downstairs. Larry was standing in the lobby.

"Larry, can you do me a favor? Will you get a message to the sheriff?"

"Sure thing, Butch," Larry said. "What is it?"

"Tell him we've got a lead on the kidnapped woman," she said, "and the bank robber. We'll meet him at his office in two hours."

Larry nodded. "Got it."

Butch walked out of the hotel. She motioned to the stable boy.

"I need to run across the street, but I'll be right back," she said. "Please have Rosey ready."

He nodded and hurried back into the stable.

She ran across the road and down a bit to Agica's house. She knocked on the door and went inside before she got an answer.

"Please be home, please be home," she whispered as she strode to the back room.

"Butch, what's going on?" Agica was still sitting behind the desk. "I haven't gotten out to the ranch. Got stuck here doing research for someone."

"I need you to stop everything," Butch said. "I apologize for earlier. But now I need you to find me any death records from April 1883 for a Sarah Jane Baranco, or Sarah Jane McShane."

"I've got the newspapers from back then," she said. "Come on."

Butch followed her to the back of the house where she had the newspaper morgue. Agica flipped through stacks of newspapers. Butch had been back here with her before when they looked through all of 1882, trying to find some notice of her mother's death.

"I've looked at 1883 before," Aggie said. "I remember a teacher dying, along with her daughter. It was quite tragic. Suicide. Here. April 1883. There was an article on it."

Butch moved closer and looked down at the yellow paper to where Aggie's finger was.

"Authorities discovered the body of Sarah J. McShane Baranco hanging from a rope down near the river late Sunday evening," Butch read out loud. "Although Mrs. Baranco did not leave a suicide note, the sheriff believes she took her own life. Authorities also believe Mrs. Baranco's two-year-old daughter AnnaBella has also died, either by accident or foul play. Her bassinet was found empty and destroyed downstream. The sheriff tells us they found cat prints at the site which they believe belong to the infamous Jezebel jaguar who has a distinctive scar on her left paw. In addition to the prints, they discovered blood and human hair. The sheriff has send out a group of hunters to find the jaguar. Mrs. Baranco's kin have been notified."

Butch felt dizzy. She closed her eyes. She was looking down

at her tiny hands. Blood was everywhere. Someone was cursing. Grandma No One. She saw pieces of her hair floating to the ground.

"I had forgotten I used to get these wicked bloody noses when I was a girl," Butch said. "I could be calm and collected and no one would know I was afraid or anything, and then I'd get a bloody nose. Sister Claw said it was god's judgment against me. And Grandma Crow or Grandma No One used to cut my hair down to my scalp, for years. People didn't know I was a girl for a long, long time. I bet Grandma No One took me, and then Grandma Crow kept me."

"Butch, what are you talking about?" Agica glanced at the paper and then looked at her. "Are you saying you are Anna-Bella Baranco? This dead school teacher was your mother?"

Butch nodded.

"Oh my word," Aggie said. "I'm sorry. I saw the obituary—not this article—when you had me look years ago, but I never put two and two together. I mean, it was a mother and a daughter dead. Even if I'd read this article I wouldn't have known it was you."

"Aggie," Butch said. "It's not your fault. We'll talk about this later. I gotta go."

She hurried out of the house and across the road. She saw George standing next to Rosey and Bucket. She was so glad to see him she wanted to kiss him.

"George!" she called.

He looked over at her. He smiled. She grinned. Almost always he looked glad to see her.

She gave him a quick embrace. "George, thanks so much for coming."

"What's going on?"

Butch put her face in Rosey's neck and hugged her. She smelled good. Just like horse. Then Butch stepped back, took the reins, and got up on her. George mounted Bucket, and they started riding out of town.

"I found the kidnapped woman," Butch said.

"You've found the woman?" George asked.

"You will not fucking believe it," Butch said. "Yes, I found the kidnapped woman and the bank robber. You were right about Mateo Cruz all along. There was definitely something wrong with him."

George looked at her. "What? Tell me."

She grinned. "Man, I am so glad to see you. I was thinking we should hang some pictures in the casita, or something. Make it look more like a home, at least until you go off and get married."

"What are you grinning about?"

"Mateo Cruz is Adriana de la Baranco."

"What?" he said. "Who is Adriana Baranco?"

"She's the woman who robbed the bank saying that someone had her in his crosshairs. There was no him. No sniper. Adriana dressed as a man to come here and get her son and take him away. And more than that, Adriana is my sister. Her father is my father." She reached into her front pocket but the cameo and the pendant were gone. Her fingers touched the bullet. "Dang. I left them at the hotel."

"You better start from the beginning," George said.

Butch shook her head. "Oh man, the beginning was before I was born. My mother wasn't a prostitute. She was a school teacher who got pregnant and then married the father, the man she loved. She got depressed, though, especially after his parents disinherited him and they were broke. Then he left for a time and her melancholy got worse and she killed herself. When he came back to town, they told him his wife had killed herself and his daughter, too. Me. I was that daughter."

As they headed back to Wayward, Butch told George all she

knew. He barely said a word. He seemed more shocked than she was.

Butch was shocked.

She was also giddy.

Her entire life had just changed.

Or at least her view of her entire life had changed.

When they rode into Wayward, hardly anyone was around. Hunter sat out back with Jimmy. Butch called them over as she and George got off the horses.

The kids ran over to them.

"Jimmy, do me a favor," Butch said. She was asking a lot of favors today. "Saddle up Mateo's horse and have it ready right away." He nodded and went into the stable. "Hunter, I need to borrow a dress and probably some undergarments from you. A petticoat or whatever it is girls wear. Do you have anything like that?"

George and Hunter both looked at her.

"Not for me," she said. "Hell hasn't frozen over."

"I have a couple dresses," Hunter said.

"Nothing fancy," Butch said. "In fact, probably something you don't mind parting company with."

"Okay," Hunter said.

"Where is Mateo?"

"He's up in his room," Hunter said.

"You run and get that stuff for me and then come get me," Butch said. "We'll be in Mateo's room."

"All right," Hunter said. "Aren't you going to ask me about Herman?"

"Herman?" Oh yes. Herman. "Sure, how's Herman?"

Hunter frowned. "He's fine. He's ready to show you what he did with those things."

"Tomorrow," Butch said. "He can show me during the Spectacle, if that will work."

"Sure," Hunter said. "That will be very appropriate."

The three of them went into the house. Butch waved to Maria, TomA, and Patrick. Hunter ran down the hall and away from them, toward her room. George and Butch went up the stairs until they reached the top floor. Butch walked to the closed door and knocked.

"Come in," Mateo said.

Butch opened the door and walked into the small room. Mateo sat up in bed and smiled. Then Mateo saw George, and he—she—got up.

"I need to know one thing from you," Butch said. "If you lie to me one more time from here on, I will take you to the sheriff's office myself and turn you over to him."

Mateo swallowed.

"Did you shoot Deputy Jones?" Butch asked.

"I never did," she said.

"Where's the money?"

"In a cave, not far from town," Mateo said.

Hunter came into the room, holding a blue cotton dress and a petticoat.

"Thanks, Hunter," Butch said. She took the clothing from Hunter. "Now you should leave. I don't want you to hear the rest of this."

The girl nodded and did as she was told. George closed the door behind her.

"I know you are Adriana de la Baranco," Butch said. "I've met your father. I have convinced him to bring your son back to you. You won't be forced to marry anyone, but you have to stop acting like such an asshole. You're a grown woman with a son. You need to act responsibly."

"Who are you to talk to me this way?" Adriana said.

Butch glanced at George and then at Adriana.

"I am your big sister," she said. "Now here's what we're

gonna do. The deputy thinks a man kidnapped you. George and I are supposed to be looking for that kidnapped woman. We're gonna find you, along with all the money. You're going to say that the bank robber tied you up and left you there and never came back and you don't know where he is. You're going to act like you're glad to see your father. Once the bank has back all the money, they're not going to be so concerned with tracking down the bank robber. You'll be free to be with your son instead of serving life in prison for bank robbery. Are you willing to do this?"

"I—I guess," she said.

"Then let's go," Butch said. "You'll be Mateo Cruz, just a friend helping us out, and then Mateo Cruz will continue on his way and we will find Adriana de la Baranco in the cave with the money. Don't tell anyone you were Mateo Cruz. Got it?"

She nodded.

"What did you mean when you said you were my big sister?" she asked. "My sister died before I was born."

"News of my death was a tad premature," Butch said. "But we'll talk about that later."

Butch, Adriana (as Mateo), and George left the house and the Wayward Ranch without talking to anyone else. They headed to the cave. Butch knew which one Adriana was talking about; she should have thought to look in it before. It wasn't far from Crazy Betty's house and where the deputy had been killed.

It was a strange ride, the three of them, on the three horses. Butch felt like everything was suffused with gold, as though she was in a dream. She couldn't quite see right or hear right. Adriana kept asking her questions, but Butch told her it would all have to wait.

Wait, wait, wait.

Butch thought she heard someone singing, "Bella, Bella, Bella."

She could see the pendant swinging in the air. Her tiny hand reached for it.

She saw the blood again, the hair, sensed her mother hanging, swinging. Her tiny hand reached for her.

When they got to the cave, hidden behind a copse of birch trees, the three dismounted. In the past, wild animals had made this little cave—this hole in the earth—their home. Butch looked around and saw no people, not even any houses in the distance. She and George made noises near the cave to scare out any animals.

Then the three of them ducked down and went into the cave. Adriana moved ahead of them to the back, about six feet from the opening. Butch heard the rustle of leaves but couldn't see anything in the dark.

"It's gone," Adriana said. "The money is gone."

"What?" Butch said.

"How can you see anything?" George asked. A moment later he struck a match. The cave momentarily lit up, showing cobwebs, dried leaves, some kind of animal scat, and the three of them.

"Fuck," Butch said. "Did anyone see you come in here?"

"I don't think so," Adriana said. "But I don't know. Those deputies were after me. I had to stash the stuff somewhere. I figured no one would come in here. Seemed pretty scary to me."

George and Butch looked at one another. Butch rolled her eyes. "City girl."

"I am not!" she said. "Now what are we going to do?"

They walked out of the cave.

"Hello there!" Butch recognized Crazy Betty's voice, although she couldn't see her yet. "Space touristas, is that you?"

In another moment, Crazy Betty came around the corner with a saddlebag slung over her shoulder.

"Have ye come looking for this?" she asked. "I saw you hide

it after ye fell to the Earth. I kept it fer you. I've been waiting for ye to come back."

"Those are the saddlebags," Adriana whispered.

"Cra—I mean, Betty, hello," Butch said. "It's me, Butch."

Crazy Betty came closer. "I see you there, Butch. I've been hoping you'd come by. I figured I could trust you with this. You'd give it to the space touristas when they needed it. Ambrose Bierce told me a long time ago you could always be trusted." She lifted the saddlebags off her shoulder. George took them from her and handed them to Butch. Butch handed them to Adriana. She opened the bags and looked inside. Then she nodded to Butch.

"I'm sorry I didn't come over sooner," Butch said. "We've had a lot going on."

"I understand," Crazy Betty said. "Ever since the space touristas have come, I've been hearing noises every night. I was going to leave the stuff here where you put it, little alien girl."

Butch glanced at George. Crazy Betty knew Adriana was a woman, but neither of them had guessed?

"I stood watch that night ye came," Crazy Betty said. "But I heard the coyotes out here sniffing around and arguing. I got as close as I could and I shot in their direction, you know, just so as to frighten them away, but I decided then and there that I better take these saddlebags into my house, which is eternally protected because of Ambrose's friendship with the space touristas. I've kept the bags since and been watching for yer return."

"Thank you so much, madam," Adriana said.

Adriana got the dress and underwear from Butch's saddlebags, and then she went into the cave and disappeared from sight.

Butch looked at Crazy Betty.

"Betty, can you show me exactly where you were standing and in which direction you pointed your rifle?"

"Sure, I kin show ye," she said.

Crazy Betty walked away from the cave and the trees and out into the scrub a ways. George and Butch followed. Crazy Betty put an imaginary rifle on her shoulder, closed one eye, and pulled the trigger. George and Butch followed the trajectory. George stayed by Crazy Betty; Butch walked into the desert, pretending she was the bullet.

She stopped—landed—right where the deputy had fallen.

She looked back at Crazy Betty who grinned and gave her a thumbs up.

"Oh crap," Butch said.

Butch walked back to Crazy Betty. George looked grim. He understood.

"Betty, you can't shoot at the coyotes any more," Butch said.

"Why?"

"Because you could kill one of them," Butch said.

"Naw," she said. "You can't kill no coyote with a bullet. Coyotes are immortal."

"They aren't," Butch said. "And sometimes they are disguised space touristas. What if you shot and killed one of them?"

"That would be terrible," she said. "Might piss off Ambrose. Then he'd never come back and do the wild with me." She winked at Butch. "Wouldn't want to risk that."

"Will you remember?" Butch said. "You can't shoot at coyotes. You can't shoot at anything at all. Promise?"

Crazy Betty shrugged. "I'll try to remember."

"What if I take your gun?" Butch said.

"No! Ye can't take my gun," Crazy Betty said. "I need that fer protection. Ye can take my bullets though." She nodded. "Yep. That'll work."

Adriana came out of the cave wearing the dress. She was

beautiful, her long hair out of the pony tail now, her face dirty from cave dust.

Crazy Betty smiled.

"See how they can change their skin just like that," she said. "It's almost like how we change our clothes."

"Almost," Butch said.

They went to Betty's house and got all of her bullets. Butch would have to remember to go around town and make certain no one sold her any more ammunition.

Then Butch, George, and Adriana headed for town and the sheriff's office.

It was near night by the time they got there.

The sheriff and Deputy Fargo stood on the porch watching them as they rode up. Hector de la Baranco held the hand of a little boy.

Soon, George, Butch, and Adriana were at the office. The little boy cried "Mama!" and ran to Adriana the second after she dismounted. Hector followed his grandson, and the three of them embraced one another. The little boy cried. Butch felt a little teary-eyed herself.

George handed Sheriff Carter the saddlebags full of money.

"We found her and the cash in a cave not far from where the deputy was shot," Butch said. "She said the bank robber left her there and never came back."

"Can you give us a description of him?" Deputy Fargo asked.

"I didn't see him," Adriana said. "He wore a mask every time he was around me."

Butch raised an eyebrow. A nice touch. She hoped the deputy believed her.

"My daughter has been through a terrible ordeal," Hector said. "I'm so grateful to you all for finding her. And I am glad the bank will get back its money."

"Deputy Jones is still dead," Fargo said.

"The woman is safe," Sheriff Carter said, "and the money is returned. We can't do anything for Deputy Jones except look for his killer. Why don't you take your daughter back to the hotel?"

Hector glanced at Butch. She nodded. Then he put his arm around Adriana's waist and the three of them walked away, toward the hotel. Butch had hardly gotten a glimpse of her new nephew.

"I'm sorry about your partner," Butch said to Fargo. "I wish we could have helped more with that."

Fargo nodded. "I appreciate that. I better get this money back to the bank. Then we'll figure out what to do next."

He turned to go back into the sheriff's office. Carter walked back over to Rosey and Bucket with George and Butch.

"That kind of wrapped up quick and easy," Carter said.

"It's a long story," Butch said. "It was Crazy Betty who shot Jones, on accident. She thought she was getting off a warning shot to some coyotes. We've confiscated her bullets. Maybe you could get her rifle from her. She doesn't know what she did. Wouldn't do anybody any good if she went to jail."

"Butch, we don't make those kinds of decisions," Carter said.

"Come on," Butch said. "She'd die in a prison. She wasn't trying to kill anyone. She had no malice in her heart."

"Just craziness," Carter said. "I can't have Fargo and the rest of them out trying to find this killer when we know who it is. They might end up hurting someone else."

"How about this," George said. "A few days after Fargo leaves, you can wire them that you found a body out in the desert and you found some of Adriana's belongings with it. You're certain it's the robber."

Carter shook his head. "One lie on top of another."

"We all have lies we're keeping track of," Butch said. "I remember a certain amount of evidence that got lost about the time your son—"

Carter waved his hand. "We don't need to start listing our various adventures together through the years. I see your point. I'll have a talk with Betty, about getting her guns from her. And I'm sure something or someone will show up dead in the desert in the next few days."

"Could be a raccoon," Butch said. "Or a coyote. Not that I'm wishing death on any of them."

"Shit," Carter said. "Get on out of here before I change my mind."

"I'll tell you something that'll tickle your funny bone," Butch said as she went around Rosey and then put her left foot in the stirrup. "That man you just met: He's my daddy. Well, either him or Ambrose Bierce, but I'm leaning more towards him."

"What?"

"I'll tell you all about it later."

Carter looked over at George. George smiled and got on Bucket.

"See you at the Wayward Art Spectacle!" Butch said.

She and George rode out of town.

Ten

Butch woke up early the next morning. She yawned and stretched.

Then she remembered she had a family now. A blood family. A sister. Father. Nephew.

A sister who seemed a bit unbalanced. A father who was a bit controlling. And who knew what the kid was like?

The night before, Butch sat down her Wayward family and told them the whole story about Adriana and Hector. She even told them about her own child. About Zachary.

She didn't tell them Adriana was really Mateo Cruz. No sense making them part of that story, just in case it ever unraveled.

TomA immediately sent an invitation to Hector, Adriana, and Frederico to come stay at the house.

Now it was just after dawn. Butch could hear people outside finishing up preparations for the art spectacle.

Butch got out of bed, pulled on her jeans, and ran her hands through her hair. Then she went out into the kitchen. George was sitting at the table drinking coffee. She put her hand on his shoulder as she passed. He put his hand over hers for a moment. She stopped, stayed still. Then he let go. She sat across from him.

"Did you see Marco hung one of his pieces from the piñon tree?" George said. "They're carved birds. All kinds of bright colors. I swear as I walked by them last night they were singing."

Butch smiled and took the cup of coffee from George's hands. She drank a little and then handed it back to him.

"They probably were singing," Butch said. "Probably took one look at you, George, and fell in love. *George.* Is that really your name?"

"You mean is it my tribal name?" George asked. "The name my family gave to me?" He shook his head. "It's my name now. It means nothing. True names need to be secret, only known to the wind, trees, clouds, sun, and moon. Is AnnaBella your real name?"

Butch smiled. "Bella. I like that. I used to wish that was my name. Maybe I was remembering." She shrugged. "Who knows? I know your true name, George. Your true name is friend. Friend and brother. I know I've been a real prick some of the time. But my asshole days are over. I'm gonna be a better friend."

"You've always been a good friend," George said. "Don't go rewriting history."

"I'm sorry I gave away Zachary without talking to you about it," she said. "I was such a kid. I had no idea what I was doing. I had no idea who you were in my life. I didn't know you would be my closest friend. I didn't know that you would be the person I loved most in the world for the rest of my life."

George looked at his coffee and then up into Butch's eyes. They gazed at one another until George smiled.

"You should marry that girl if you want to," Butch said. "I'm behind you. I'll support you, whatever you do. Well, not whatever you do. Say you decided to jump off a cliff. I would not be behind you on that. Or if you wanted to dance into a nest of rattlesnakes. Naw, I wouldn't go there either. So except for a few hundred exceptions, I'm right behind you, supporting you."

"Oh my god, shut up. Don't we have work to do? Really hard work so that you'll have to stop talking."

Butch grinned and stood. She stretched.

"Ain't nuthin' gonna keep me from yakking away," she said. "Not even your sweet gorgeous face."

George groaned. "Save me now."

Visitors began arriving soon after breakfast. Butch was on alert for thieves or hustlers, as usual during the Spectacle, but she also enjoyed the art and the visitors. She liked walking over the grounds and seeing art everywhere: paintings, sculptures, pottery, glass, jewelry.

This year someone had made a green dragon from found metal pieces. Someone else had created a bunch of large boxes (made from who knew what), painted them bright colors, and then piled them in one of the horse pastures. They looked like building blocks for a giant child.

Paintings hung from trees and inside the house on various walls. Some of them depicted real scenes, especially from the area, the Blood Mountains, the aspens, cottonwoods, piñons, wildflowers, horses. Houses. Some were of places real and imaginary.

This year some artists had strung many of their smaller creations onto string and then hung them together from trees, like the birds George had told Butch about. In another tree, tiny jaguars, mountain lions, and lynxes twirled in the wind. In another tree, horses. Still another, tiny people. Butch stared at the people. She squinted. That one looked like George. That one Hunter. TomA. Was that her?

Beautiful quilts covered bushes, hung from branches, and stretched across the ground.

People brought food, but Maria had put out an amazing spread. Table were filled with enchiladas, tamales, frijoles, beans, roasted chicken, roasted pork, prickly pear pads, and on and on.

Fortunately Butch had regained her appetite.

She lost a little of it when Angel arrived on Merle T. Connelly's arm. Angel wore her clothes all proper, without a hint of bosom showing.

Then Marigold arrived. She was dressed in a dark gold dress. She smiled and waved when she saw Butch. Butch went over to her.

"Don't you look gorgeous," Marigold said. "That blue shirt looks good on you."

Butch kissed her on the cheek, and Marigold put her arm through Butch's.

"I bet you the blue shirt looks better off me," Butch whispered.

Marigold laughed. "Come on over later and let me see."

"I have a lot to tell you," Butch said.

"I look forward to it," Marigold said. She smiled and then wandered away.

Butch's heart skipped a bit when Hector arrived with Adriana and Frederico. Adriana was beautiful in a dark green dress. Her hair was piled up under a hat. Butch wondered if anyone would recognize her as the former Mateo Cruz. Butch wouldn't have.

Hector kissed Butch. "It is so good to see you, Bella! Let me introduce you to Frederico. Bella, this is your nephew Frederico. Rico, this is your Aunt Bella."

"Butch," she said. "You can call me Butch." She held her hand out to the boy, who shyly shook it. His eyes looked violet.

His hair was black. His skin olive-colored.

"I like Aunt Bella," he said. "It means beautiful, like you."

Butch laughed.

"It is nice to see you again, sister," Adriana said. "I've been jealous of the dead you all my life. Now I'll get to be jealous of the living you."

"Nothing to be jealous of," Butch said. "I'm just a poor country person trying to do the best I can."

Adriana smiled. Hector laughed. "You sound just like your mother! How I miss her."

"My mother will be glad to hear that," Adriana said.

"Your mother knows I loved Sarah Jane with all my heart," he said.

"And that explains why you never loved Mother," Adriana said. "Come, Rico. Let's look at the pretty glass."

She walked away with her son.

"She is very grateful to you," Hector said. "She needs time. It's all a shock."

"It's a shock to me, too," Butch said. "And to you. I can't imagine I'm what you expected in a daughter."

"I didn't expect anything," he said. "I thought you were dead! Now I don't care about anything except that you are alive."

"You don't want to try and marry me off, too?"

He smiled. "I think I have learned my lesson."

"Aren't you rich?"

He nodded. "I suppose."

"How have you survived the Mexican revolution?"

"Oh, that is a long story," he said. "Let us say I have friends in many places, high and low. And I definitely supported and support reform. But that is a tale for another time. Please, will you come home with me to Mexico? I'd like you to meet the rest of the family."

Butch looked around. Maria stood by the tables talking to

Trick. They both looked up and smiled at her. Over by the casita George and TomA talked. They watched her, too. TomA smiled and waved. She knew he wanted to come over and introduce himself to Hector. And Jimmy and Hunter were standing too close to one another by the chicken house.

"This is my home," Butch said. "These people are my family."

"I understand that," Hector said. "But now you have a family of the blood, too. I can make your life a lot easier. I can buy you land. Give you a house. You could be a woman of leisure."

Butch shook her head. "There's nothing I need or want," she said. "At least not right now."

"Some day, some time, I would love to come visit you," Butch said, "as long as I'm welcome."

"Of course," he said. "Of course. Here." He lifted something from his vest pocket: the cameo. "I kept the pendant, since it was mine, but this I give back to you. It was always intended for you."

Butch took the cameo from him.

"Thank you, Pops," she said, and she kissed his cheek.

Later Hunter took Butch to the barn. She had already saddled Rosey and her horse Palo. Herman sat on Palo.

"Herman's ready to show you," Hunter said.

"We have to ride out to it?" Butch asked. "I've got work here."

"You won't be sorry," Hunter said.

"Are you coming?" Butch asked. She did not relish being alone with the Hermit.

"Nope."

Butch got on Rosey. Herman sat hunched over on Palo. Butch sighed. He looked so weak and helpless.

"Let's go," she said.

They rode away from Wayward. Butch glanced back at the ranch. She didn't like being away during the Spectacle.

"It's not far," Herman called. He was sitting up straighter now.

Soon they were at the river.

Something shifted, felt different. Out of place. Or suddenly in place.

Herman said, "Something terrible happened here."

"Probably many terrible things," Butch said. "Prey and predators often meet at the river's edge."

They reined in the horses and looked around. The cottonwoods shaded them. The river softly gurgled over large stones in the riverbed. An old madrone, its blood red trunk smooth and opulent in this dry forest, leaned away from the cottonwood.

Butch knew this place.

"This was where my momma strung up a rope and hung herself," Butch said. She pointed. "Off that cottonwood, or so they told me. The branch must have been lower. I was nearby. By that madrone tree, actually."

Herman nodded. "Yes, I see it," he said. "I see all kinds of animals and plants here with you. A jaguar, too. Sat right over there." He pointed to a spot by the water. "The madrone watches over lost souls, you must realize. As soon as your mother left her body, she went right to that tree. Became that tree. Can't you feel her? I bet you returned here again and again and you heard stories at her feet, didn't you? At her roots. A jackrabbit sat over there, far from the jaguar. And the cottonwood tree kept the sun off you."

Butch said, "Wouldn't it have been better if the cottonwood had allowed its branch to break so that my poor mother's neck had never been broken? That would have truly helped me out."

"She would have found another place and another time," he said. "Maybe she was meant to be a tree. A madrone tree, that glorious beautiful maroon color, peaceful and beautiful in these woods alongside the stream. You should forgive her."

Butch vaguely wondered why the Hermit was talking with an Irish accent.

"I have nothing to forgive her for," Butch said. "She did what she could."

"She's not who you think she was," the Hermit said. "She's not the woman they told you she was."

"I know that now. Did Hunter tell you something about my mother?"

Herman looked over at her and shook his head. Then he got off the horse. Butch did the same. They tied up the horses, and then Herman walked away from the river, into the desert.

Butch followed.

Herman stopped and looked down.

Butch stopped and looked down.

There, spread out on the desert floor, was a kind of tiny battlefield.

Herman had taken sticks and tied them together: a long piece with a shorter piece across it, like a crucifix, only it wasn't a crucifix. It was a stick person, many stick people painted in various colors. Some of the stick people were broken and lay on the ground askew. They were red in the broken places, and red had spilled onto the ground, too.

"Did you create this?" Butch asked.

Herman nodded.

Stones and sticks and other items Butch didn't recognize had become buildings. One building resembled a church, another some kind of government building. They all had holes in them that looked like gaping wounds. How had he done that? There was Aggie's inkwell, with the ink spilled onto the ground. The black ink bled into red ink.

Not all the people were stick people. Dolls and toy soldiers were scattered here and there. Toy horses, too. Some were whole, some were not. The silver pistols lay in a tiny open grave. The whole tiny village was about six feet by three feet. Scattered throughout the village were regular sized bullets. Silver, gold, pinkish. They looked huge next to the broken stick people and toy soldiers.

Something sad, final, and chaotic about it all.

"Herman, what is this?"

"It's one of the villages where we fought," he said. "Where most of my friends died. That's the church where many of the villagers were. They thought they'd be safe in the church, but they weren't."

"Those stick figures are the dead soldiers?" Butch said.

"And the villagers," he said.

"But what's with the inkwell?"

"They sign agreements with ink, don't they? Business people and politicians decide to go to war and they sign on the dotted line. Ink is spilled and then blood is spilled."

"And the silver pistols in the grave?"

"My hopes that we could bury all weapons."

"And the bullets?" Butch said. "They're bigger than everything because they can end all life?"

Herman nodded.

"I know I have to take all the items back," he said. "I didn't think I was stealing. I thought they were discards. Things people didn't use. Just like real-life soldiers. And these villagers. Expendable."

"It's beautiful," Butch said, "and awful. You should have made it part of the Spectacle."

"It already is a spectacle, isn't it?"

"I'm sorry you had a terrible time," Butch said. "Can you let it go, forget about it? Or at least . . . transcend it."

Herman looked at her. "Can you?"

"I wasn't in a war," she said.

"But you were," he said.

She thought about how she had to steel herself every day to prevent some kind of onslaught from the boys, or from the nuns.

And then later with Grandma No One.

"I guess a lot of us have some kind of war in our past," Butch said.

She heard a growl.

She looked around.

She saw desert, the cottonwood tree by the stream, and Herman. Herman was watching her.

"Did you hear anything?" she asked.

Herman shook his head.

Butch looked down. She saw the bullets. And something on the bullets.

She crouched down and picked up one of the bullets.

Someone had scratched an "X" in the middle of the bullet. Only it wasn't exactly an "X." It was a "t." Butch took the cub bullet from her pocket and held it up next to the unspent bullet.

"I'll be," she said. It was a "t" not an "X" scored into the bullet that had killed the jaguar cub.

"Herman, do you know where you got these bullets? The ones with the markings on them?"

"Sure," he said. "I got them with the silver pistols. I liked the markings. They were on the night stand at Angel's."

"That motherfucker," Butch said.

"What is it?" Herman asked.

Butch grabbed a couple more bullets and put them in her pocket.

"I've got to run back to the ranch," she said. "You all right on your own?"

Herman nodded.

Butch ran to Rosey. She untied her, jumped on her, and they galloped toward the ranch. Butch felt every cell in her body vibrating with anger and righteous indignation.

In no time it seemed, they were at the gates to Wayward. Butch stopped Rosey so that she wasn't galloping into a crowd of people. Jimmy and Hunter saw her, and they ran to get Rosey. Butch dismounted, handed the reins over to Hunter and then she strode through the crowd until she saw Merle T. Connelly standing by one of the food tables with Angel.

Everyone looked up at Butch.

Must have sensed her urgency. Or her anger.

"Merle T. Connelly?" she said.

He looked up at her. She walked over to him. She wanted to hit him so badly. She wished she had her pistols so she could shoot him. But she wasn't wearing them. Never wore them during the Spectacle.

"What do you want, McLean?" Merle asked.

She took the unspent bullets out of her shirt pocket.

"These yours?" she asked.

George came up to her. She handed him one of the bullets. Then she handed Merle the others.

Merle looked at them. He smiled. "Yes, these are mine. Did you find the thief who stole them? I mark all of mine with a 't' so that I know when my bullet hits the mark. Which is pretty much always."

The crowd chuckled. If a crowd can chuckle.

Sheriff Carter came and stood next to Butch. Smart man, he knew something was up.

She pulled out the spent bullet and showed it to Carter. George handed him the unspent bullet Butch had just given him. The sheriff looked at both bullets.

"Looks like the same marking to me," Carter said.

He handed the spent bullet to Merle.

Merle looked at them and shrugged. "Yeah, this looks like mine."

Man, Butch wanted to smash in his face.

Or scream at him that he had no right to plant his flag in her particular field, so to speak.

She looked at Angel who seemed confused.

Not that Angel was *her* field.

Butch snatched the spent bullet back from Merle.

"George, would you mind telling these good folks where we found that spent bullet?" Butch said. She held the bullet up in the air.

"We found this in the body of the dead jaguar cub," he said. "The one that Butch supposedly accidentally killed when she was a girl."

Merle's eyes widened. "Now what a minute," he said. "Everyone knows Butch did that killin'."

"We remember you being there that day," George said. "You rode through, hell bent for leather."

TomA said, "You let Butch bear the weight of that tragedy all these years when you were the one who really killed that cub?"

"She never believed she did it," Merle said. "Besides, nothing weighs on her, not even the fact that her whore of a mother strung herself up and killed herself rather than spend another day with her."

Angel slapped him across the face.

People gasped. Even Butch.

It wasn't so much a slap as a slug.

"Don't you dare say such a thing," Angel said.

Butch glanced over at her father. Adriana had her hand on his arm, restraining him.

"You better say something here," George said, "or else

you're gonna be in a whole lot of trouble."

"I was hunting Jezebel," Merle said. "Thought I'd be a hero if I could finally take her down. Something happened and I missed. Or I mistook the cub for her. It happened so fast. And then I ran out of there. I was hoping I was wrong, and when they started saying it was Butch's fault, I figured I must have gotten it wrong." He shrugged. "It could have happened."

"You knew you killed that cub," Butch said. "And you were out stalking Jezebel for no other reason except your own need to be grandiose? That's disgusting, Merle."

Everyone was watching her. She saw Agica near the back of the crowd. She held up her pistol. Butch shook her head.

No, there would be no bloodletting here today.

"You need to make restitution to the mother of the cub," Butch said to Merle. "To Jezebel."

"How would I do that?" he asked.

"We should all go up there with you," Maria said. "To the grave of the cub. We will leave offerings and sing songs. Then you will stay there all night, Merle. If Jezebel does not eat you in the night, then she has forgiven you, and you may return to our community."

"I'm not going to sit on some mountain waiting for a jaguar to come eat me," Merle said.

"Or forgive you," Butch said.

"It's either that or we charge you with harming an endangered animal," Carter said.

"There ain't no such law," Merle said.

"There should be," Angel said. "I ain't ever gonna let you near me again, Merle T. Connolly, now that I know what a coward you are. Chances are you could get some other woman to come your way someday, but only if you go up that mountain. Otherwise, we'll make sure everyone knows you're a coward."

"Rather be a coward than dead," Merle said.

"That mean you believe Jezebel is a supernatural being, bent on revenge?" Butch asked.

Merle looked at her. She stared at him.

"All right," he said.

Three days later, after the Spectacle was over, a large group of people rode out and up, following Butch and George to the grave of the jaguar cub. Adriana stayed in town with Frederico, but Hector came, along with Agica, Hunter, Maria, Jimmy, Patrick, Marigold, and others.

Merle was not amongst the others.

They heard Merle had ridden out of town in the dark of night.

No one expected to see him again.

They got off their horses at the bottom of the ridge. Those who could climbed up the ridge and ducked into the woods where it was dark and quiet.

Some of them had brought drums and rattles.

Maria led them.

They made noise and they made music.

The wind wound through the trees. Butch could hear growls in-between their songs.

Maria whispered to the wind, to the sun, the moon, the stones, to the trees, the clouds, birds, animals, insects. To the dirt under their feet. Maria asked for blessings for everything and everyone.

Butch looked over at George. He smiled. Butch and George had said blessings over the grave before, but this was nice. She looked over at her father. He seemed completely at home here with these people and this place. No wonder her mother had loved him.

"We ask for forgiveness from Jezebel, the jaguar mother," Maria said. "One of our own took your son's life. It was a mistake. We make restitution here tonight, with our song and our offerings of food."

Just then they heard the sound of footsteps. They all turned around.

Merle T. Connelly was walking toward them.

No one said anything. They made a place in the circle for him as everyone moved one way or another.

They sang more. Other people said prayers. Made offerings. One by one, they left the graveside.

Until only George, Butch and Merle remained.

Merle was shaking.

"I have to stay here all night?" he asked.

Butch shrugged. "That's what Maria said."

"What does she know?"

"She knows everything," George said. "Especially about this land."

"Do you want me to stay with you?" Butch asked.

She couldn't believe she had said those words out loud.

He nodded. "Yes, please."

Butch looked over at George. He shook his head and rolled his eyes.

"I need to check with Maria," Butch said. She and George left Merle next to the grave. Then Butch went down to the ridge. Nearly everyone else was ready to ride out.

"Maria," Butch said. "Can I stay with Merle through the night?"

"Down here," Maria said. "You can have a fire and stay here. But he remains up in the woods. I saw it in a dream." Maria got on her horse. "I'm getting too old for this."

"Thanks," Butch said.

Maria nodded. She turned her horse around and led the group away.

Butch's father walked his horse over to Butch.

"I'm taking Adriana and Rico home tomorrow," Hector said to Butch. "Should I wait for you?"

Butch shook her head. "No," she said. "Go on home to Mexico. Keep in touch though."

"I will be back soon," he said.

"Is that a promise?" she asked.

He sighed. "That is the same thing your mother asked. The last thing. I promised her and I promise you. I will be back soon."

Butch nodded. He reached his hand down to her. She took his hand and squeezed it. Then she let it go.

"Thanks, Pops," she said. "Tell Adriana and Rico adios for me."

Butch went back up the ridge to the jaguar cub grave.

"I'll be down at the bottom of the ridge," she told Merle. "You can do this. Make amends. Talk to her. Do whatever you need to do to prove you aren't a worthless piece of shit."

"But what if that is what I am?"

Butch looked down at him.

"Aw, Merle," she said. "No one is a worthless piece of shit."

She and George went back down the ridge. It was starting to get dark.

"You don't have to stay," Butch said to George.

"Who says I'm gonna stay?" he said. He began looking around for firewood. "I'm just tired. I want to rest for a bit."

"Truly," Butch said. "I brought my mother's tatters box. I was going to look through the contents again. Maybe stop by Grandma Crow's place and look for the suicide note. You know, good times."

"You want me to leave," he said, "I'll leave."

Butch watched him. How familiar his movements were. How graceful he was.

"Naw," she said. "You know what? I don't believe Grandma No One. There wasn't any suicide note. Just her way of driving me crazy. Man, I'm about done in. Entertain me with some stories so I can get some sleep."

George laughed. "You've heard all my stories."

Butch nodded. "Yep. And I want to hear them again."

They built a fire, talked a while, then got out their sleeping rolls.

"I'm thinking about going on a trip," George said. "Down to Mexico, deep into the mountains. I've heard there are things to see there. It's supposed to be amazing."

"More amazing than these mountains?" she asked.

"Maybe," he answered.

"You should do it," Butch said. "Whatever you want to do, you should do it. I want you to have everything you've ever wanted."

George didn't say anything.

"Wouldn't mind going back East either," George said.

"I asked Aggie to look up Zachary's grandma," Butch said. "Turns out they're some rich family. I mean rich rich. I wonder if they would consider me acceptable now that I have a rich father? Not that I give a shit what they think."

"Can't see you rich," George said. "You gonna start wearing dresses?"

"If I do, shoot me," she said. "It means the space touristas have gotten to me."

George chuckled.

After a while he fell to sleep. Butch sat by the dying fire listening to the night. She kept wondering when Merle would come running out of the woods. She didn't have much confidence that he would spend the night.

She thought about getting out the tatters box.

Decided against it.

She fell to sleep.

Dreamed Jezebel walked around the fire snorting fire.

Or maybe she licked Butch's face.

She awakened near dawn.

Cat prints ringed their campsite.

Couldn't tell if they were Jezebel's or not.

George and Butch looked at the prints and then up at the ridge.

"Wonder if he made it through the night?" Butch asked.

"Only one way to find out," George said.

"Aw, I don't like carcasses that animals have chewed on," Butch said. "Makes me queasy. Got to be another way."

"Hey, Connelly!" George yelled.

Butch laughed. "I guess there was another way," she said.

"Connelly!"

A few moments later, Merle emerged from the woods, looking no worse for wear.

"Yeah?"

"You dead?" George asked.

"Don't think so," he said.

"Then get your ass down here," George said. "I'm cold, tired, and hungry. And you're buying."

They broke camp and then headed down the mountain. Merle talked almost nonstop about all the animal sounds he had heard in the night. He was certain Jezebel had been right there with him, ready to kill him, but he had stood his ground.

George and Butch looked at each other every once in a while.

When the hell was he going to shut up?

They came to the cut off to Grandma Crow's house, but they went past it.

Then they came to the river.

Butch pulled Rosey to a stop.

"I'm gonna stay here for a bit," Butch said. "I've got a letter to write."

George looked at her. She pressed her lips together. He nodded.

"A letter?" Merle said. "Way out here? I thought I was buying you breakfast?"

"Connelly, if you don't shut the hell up I'm gonna shoot you myself," George said.

The two of them rode off. Butch walked Rosey alongside the river for a while. When she recognized the cottonwood and the madrone, she stopped Rosey and got off her. She tied her up. Then she took the tatters box from the saddlebags. She went to the river and looked down at the clear water for a while. Then she sat under the madrone tree. She set the tatters box on the ground in front of her. Then she leaned over to open it.

It wouldn't open.

She frowned.

She had opened it the day before when she returned the cameo to it and added a couple sheets of stationary and a pencil.

Probably when she dropped it the other day something had gotten off-balance.

She tried to open it again but the latch was stuck.

She picked it up.

And the bottom fell out, along with a single sheet of paper.

"Oh man," she said.

How could she be so careless?

Wait.

Why hadn't everything fallen out?

She held the box up and looked under it.

There was another bottom.

Her heart started racing.

The tatters box had a false bottom?

She picked up the sheet of paper.

It had writing on it: her mother's handwriting.

"Dear Bella," the letter began.

Butch put her hand to her mouth.

What?

"Dear Bella, this is your mama. I want to tell you first, there are no answers here. I'm sorry. Today is the last day of my life, and I spent it with you. What joy! You were good company as always. I wonder how you can bear to be with me now that I am so sad. My sister will come get you soon. I am timing this just so. She will be here, after I go to the other world. She will keep you safe until your poppa comes. I hope he knows I love him. He is a good man. His parents are not so good. Or at least, they are not very kind. They have assured me that they will find a way to annul our marriage and make you a bastard and me— Oh, this is not what I wanted to write. I wanted to tell you that I love you.

"You are not to blame for any of this. I am in too much pain. I had to end it. I hope you read this when you are old enough to understand. I am not old enough.

"I am twenty-two and I feel two hundred years old, except without the wisdom of someone that old. Perhaps if I had stayed with my people, perhaps if I had been in a place where people knew me and loved me. I am your mother and I should have the answers. I don't.

"Don't blame your father. I hope you are loved. I hope you have a good family. I hope you treat yourself well.

"When I was a little girl I remember my great grandmother from Ireland would each day give us a blessing. Now I need to give you a blessing to last you the rest of your life. So I ask the spirits and the fairies to look after you. May you be blessed with the strength and presence of the mesquite tree that goes deep deep into the earth so that it may receive her constant blessing. May you be blessed with the sun on your face and a loved one always at your back. May you be blessed with fierce love that will hold you steady even when you might fall. May you be blessed with the love and blessings of the sun, moon, stars, earth, planets, the plants and animals. May you be blessed with much more wisdom than your old ma had. I wish for you so much more.

"Have a good life, darlin'!"

Butch put the paper down. She wiped the tears from her cheeks.

She looked up at the sky. One cloud floated above in the sea of blue. A breeze rustled the new leaves on the cottonwoods and aspens. Butch looked over at them, toward the river. She blinked. Near the water's edge, the old jaguar looked at her. For a moment. Then she walked into the water and disappeared. Butch blinked again. She saw her mother and father sitting by the river, kissing.

Butch wondered—for only a moment—why her mother's sister had never come for her.

She closed her eyes.

Opened them.

The madrone was whispering stories to her.

She looked up. The sky was darkening.

A bright light fell up the sky.

Hadn't that been how this all started?

She heard voices in the near distance.

She opened the lid on the tatters box. This time it opened easily. She took out a blank piece of paper and a pencil. She put her mother's letter back. Then she put the false bottom back on. She closed the lid and put the paper on it. She stared at it.

Then she wrote, "Dear Zachary."

She couldn't write, "This is your mama," like her mother had.

"Dear Zachary, I trust that someone has told you about me.

I am your mama. I live in a small town in New Mexico. I will enclose the address. I would like to meet you and so would the man who helped me give birth to you."

That didn't sound exactly right, but she wasn't going to try to erase it.

How could she end it?

"Love."

"Sincerely?"

"Yours truly?"

She shrugged.

"Hope to hear from you soon, darlin',

"AnnaBella 'Butch' McLean McShane Baranco."

That was a good start. She'd show it to George.

Or not.

And then mail it.

She heard voices again.

She folded the piece of paper and put it back in the tatters box. Then she got up and went to Rosey.

Who had been standing there so patiently all this time.

She put the box in the saddlebag. Then she untied Rosey and they walked together toward the voices.

Butch and Rosey came out of the trees, and Butch saw George, Hunter, Herman, Agica, TomA and Patrick. They were picking up the desert. Taking apart the battlefield.

"There she is," TomA said. "We were about to come get you."

"We've got almost everything," Hunter said. "Tomorrow Herman and I will take back some of the items and give them to their rightful owners."

"I found my mother's suicide note," Butch said.

They all stopped what they were doing and looked at her.

"What did she say?" Hunter asked.

"She said that she loved me," Butch said. She hesitated, then swallowed. "And she wished for me . . . she wished for me a good life." She looked around at her friends. George nodded. "Which is exactly what I got."

Hunter grinned.

"We've got this cleaned up," TomA said. "Time to go. Maria's got supper ready. All your favorites, Butch."

"What are my favorites?" Butch asked.

"Food prepared by someone else," Patrick said.

"Oh yeah."

They all went to their horses and got on them. They started toward the ranch.

"I'm thinking I might learn to cook," Butch said.

The group moaned, collectively, everyone except Herman maybe, who didn't know her well enough.

"It could happen," Butch said.

She looked at George, who rode up next to her.

"Why do you want to learn to cook?" he asked.

"You won't be around forever," she said. "You've got mountains to climb and women to marry."

He looked at her. "I'm not going anywhere. Unless you start cooking. Then I may head for the hills."

"Fair warning," Butch said. "What about a trip to Mexico? I hear I've got some family down there."

"Sure," George said. "I'd follow you to the ends of Earth."

"To the ends of the Earth?" Butch said. "Hell. Wait until I tell my new poppa that you think Mexico is at the ends of the Earth. Might not go over well down there. At the ends of the Earth. They might send out a posse to get your mind right."

"Could they please send out a posse to get your mind right?" George said.

Butch laughed. "You always know just the right thing to say, darlin'!"

About the author

Kim Antieau has written many novels, short stories, poems, and essays. Her work has appeared in numerous publications, both in print and online, including *The Magazine of Fantasy and Science Fiction, Asimov's SF, The Clinton Street Quarterly, The Journal of Mythic Arts, EarthFirst!, Alternet, Sage Woman,* and *Alfred Hitchcock's Mystery Magazine.* She was the founder, editor, and publisher of *Daughters of Nyx: A Magazine of Goddess Stories, Mythmaking, and Fairy Tales.* Her work has twice been short-listed for the Tiptree Award, and has appeared in many Best of the Year anthologies. Critics have admired her "literary fearlessness" and her vivid language and imagination. Her first novel *The Jigsaw Woman* is a modern classic of feminist literature. She has also written *The Gaia Websters, The Fish Wife,* and *Church of the Old Mermaids.* Kim lives in the Pacific Northwest with her husband, writer Mario Milosevic. Learn more about Kim and her writing at www.kimantieau.com.

Made in the USA
Charleston, SC
30 June 2012